About the Author

Rudi Michael Jennings spent the majority of his childhood growing up in the Norfolk countryside of fields and trees, really living amongst nature and possibly giving the basis of description in his book. Through travel, various professions and a keen interest in psychology and fantasy writings, he developed a style of his very own and is keen to share it with the fantasy adventure world. This plans to be the first instalment and adventure of many to come.

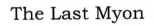

The Last Myon

Rudi Jennings

The Last Myon

Olympia Publishers
London

www.olympiapublishers.com
OLYMPIA PAPERBACK EDITION

A CIP catalogue record for this title is
available from the British Library.

ISBN: 978-1-84897-934-5

First Published in 2017

Olympia Publishers
60 Cannon Street
London
EC4N 6NP

Printed in Great Britain

Dedication

I would like to dedicate this book to my loving Fiancée, my family, my close friends (you know who you are boys) and my father who has encouraged and supported me all my life... Thanks Dad.

Chapter 1

Slowly the creaking of an old wooden cart echoed through the crudely cut path of the winter forest. Hypnotic in its rhythms with the occasional crunch of compacted snow fallen weeks ago were strangely peaceful and sombre to Ackrehm causing him to doze and sway back into his cart of meager possessions. Only the infrequent rocks hidden in snow that littered the path would make him arise for a brief moment from an almost definite ambient slumber. Therd, the mountain of a horse that could pull such a sizable cart wandered peacefully onward as if he had travelled the same path many times before and no longer required any encouragement from his master to reach their destination, always with the thought that no doubt he would be rewarded on arrival with a warm stable and a nourishing meal. Ackrehm was a Myon, an ilk of strong and honourable people that could walk upright on their hind legs creating quite a sizable adversary if ever challenged. His features were typical of a vehement Myon male, sprouting two tree like horns curving round and over their heads like the wild hill rams of this land. His face told a story of pain and hardship, dry and scarred with multiple lines like a river bed in drought or over cooked swine skin spited over a camp fire. These markings serve as an unpleasant and imposing reminder from many altercations in the past of flippant creatures wishing to test their worth against him, but as he sat cocooned in a patchy animal skin rug made from many the leftover of a true trapper, he appeared untouchable from the cold and hardships, not only from the cold this time of year, but from those of which he had become accustomed to bearing in the solitude that had become the existence of life as one of the only remaining Myon people.

Ackrehm was now sleeping soundly as his cart rolled slowly onward, perhaps the reprehensible provisions he had acquired were not as sustaining as he had hoped and sleep was the only way to conserve energy. Dreaming of a warming fire and an even more warming woman, Ackrehm was blissfully unaware of the new noises that seemed to be emanating from the ice licked branches and brushes around him ruminating from the leaves emanated like flames on dry wood. The noises were faint and almost untraceable from the heavy snorting mists expelled from the jug size nostrils' of Therd, but faint as they were, Ackrehm was not the only beast to frequent the forest on this icy winter evening, for these noises were being made by carefully placed steps in close proximity and keeping pace with the cart at all times.

A particularly loud rustle from a nearby bush caused Therd to halter and snort loudly in irritancy, but after a few seconds of silence, onward he trudged. Then the slight rustle began again and continued for at least one mile before the sounds began to interrupt Ackrehm's slumber. At first the sounds just caused rapid eye movement, but soon he began to stir and then to waken fully at the notion that the forest that seemed so safe, secluded and abandoned might be lodgings to more than just the odd owl. Pretending not to notice the extra attention something or someone was paying him, Ackrehm began to focus his post sleep vision and ready himself for possible dangers that may befall him. Therd was all too aware of the mysterious presence in the surrounding cold, but seeming to take solace in the comforting support Ackrehm placed on the reigns, letting the horse know he was awake and ready. Ever more the wagon rolled on and right alongside continued the rustling and scrambling that had followed for so long now. Ackrehm considered the fact it might be a group of some clans, young, curious and interested in a man such as himself passing through their little stretch of forest, but ever lurking in the back of his mind was the real possibility that a serious threat could be upon him at any moment; for it is spoken of by many travellers in dusky taverns of the rustling behind wagons and of narrow escapes from rogue bands of Geflacks, a dangerous species. Not because of size, but because they attack in numbers like fire ants, swarming their victims with arrow and club, tooth and claw. These fish eyed creatures are scavengers and opportunists, taking their time for an attack and usually the only reason is to loot and murder. What had made such crossing though the forest more and more treacherous, was the possible number that this sizable wilderness could harbor, for then limitless amount of creatures that burrow deep into the rich forest floors was due to the fact that the Geflacks are Hermaphrodites, having both sexual organs and reproducing in rodent-like numbers. Bands of these beasts were turning up in the most remote places, stripping the innocence from once peaceful lands, taking everything and leaving nothing but corpses and the smell of plunder in the air as thick as green ferns on a fire and twice as stomach retching.

Chapter 2

Ackrehm slowly searched with one hand behind him for something in his wagon that could be used as a makeshift weapon if in contact with would be assailants, ever-while moving on at the same pace so as not to startle whatever was following him into attack mode. One hand looped into hemp cords controlling Therd and the other sifting sneakily behind him, under rags and through baskets, for something, anything. Then catching the skin on his palm, Ackrehm stopped and without looking discovered a large nail protruding from several bundles of wood he had collected for free in the hope of fashioning a table and maybe even some chairs for his dwellings, a place he would have given anything to be at right now. Gripping with all his might, Ackrehm used his thumb and index finger to rock the nail back and forth, pulling all the while to dislodge it. After a few moments, the nail loosened and came free. Although rusty and thin it was long enough that it would surely puncture a lung or an eye if driven hard enough. So now, weapon in hand, meager as it was Ackrehm rolled on, listening to every hushed maelstrom waiting for the moment to make Therd charge and draw him to safety.

As the wagon rolled over an especially large rock and jolted down hard, bouncing Ackrehm in his seat, a snap and rushing sound occurred. Striking the reigns as hard as he could, Therd reared up in surprise and excitement with the notion of a run, but the rushing sound was to stop him dead when a section of tree came swinging rapidly from above and struck Therd hard in the side, breaking a leg and several ribs. As the horse whinnied in agony and momentum toppled him, the wagon span to the side throwing Ackrehm back into the cart and nearly somersaulting the entire vehicle. Silence; Ackrehm struggled to right himself from such a foreign position, only just managing to drag his body vertically and make his way to the front of the wagon slipping and tripping on the now uneven load, but still with nail in hand praying for Therd to be alive.

Jumping down to inspect his companion, Ackrehm stumbled slightly on what he firstly thought to be ice, but was in fact Therd's blood. A huge puddle was forming around the gallant animal as he struggled to breathe, eyes glazed and frantic from agony and the inability to move. Ackrehm crouched close by trying to calm the horse in what was obviously his last moments and still trying to figure out what on earth had occurred. The rustling started again, louder and more frantic, as if whatever it was, now had a purpose and was in full motion. Jumping to his feet, Ackrehm moved out into the path, turning as he went so as not to be surprised from behind, when he noticed movement from the rear of his crippled wagon.

'Geflacks' he sighed tightening his grip on the clearly inadequate weapon. They were swarming the wagon and making their way to the front. Therd was done for, but still Ackrehm had to resist the notion of a defensive hold or rescue as the Geflacks would surely engulf them both. Rushing from the bushes with clubs raised they attacked Therd, beating his head until his thrashing movement ceased and the snow was red and maroon like an erupting volcano. At this sight Ackrehm knew he could do nothing to save his friend, he began backing away slowly, hunched over in a childish attempt to obscure his size and so as not to attract attention. The largest and most likely leader of the attacking parasites raised the alarm of Ackrehm's whereabouts, pointing and letting out a shrill call. Like a bloodthirsty wave of darkness the Geflacks poured off the dead horse and wagon shrieking in ecstasy as they went, hurling stones that landed at Ackrehm's feet sending a mist of white powder up in to his face. Turning to run, Ackrehm was struck on the lower back by a particularly vicious throw and winced in pain, but still began making pace, bounding and striding into the woods away from danger.

The leader let out several more screams and hisses, halting the marauding bandits in their tracks, thus causing them to return to the freshly acquired wagon. Three Geflack's produced long, thin blades from pouches on their back and began the butchery process of Therd. Possibly the only reason for their attack in the first place being the sight of a large horse and that promise of such quantities of meat is not an opportunity to be missed by any such scavengers, but especially the Geflacks'. The leader raced forward to the path that Ackrehm had taken in to the forest and beckoned four others. Standing behind their Geflack leader and waiting for the order to advance, they started to unsheathe weapons. Two producing small but powerful crossbows, one a club, one a slingshot and finally, the leader produced a flail and a long dagger. Sniffing the air and bobbing his head from side to side examining the slowly darkening night-struck forest, the leader grinned yellow fangs at the sight of Ackrehm's footprints, scratched his chin that sprouted dozens of wire hairs, that were as sparse as the river bank chives, with the back of his hand, then leapt into the snow in pursuit of his escapee closely followed by the ravenous warriors of his clan.

Chapter 3

Ahead and running, weaving in between the trees trying to ignore the bitterly cold twigs that were ripping at his face, Ackrehm could hear them coming. Slipping on a fallen branch he landed hard on some rocks winding him, but as quick as Ackrehm went down, he was back on his feet running through the pain and forever thinking how he could survive what was to come. Geflack's are extremely agile mainly due to the fact that instead of two hands and two feet, they have four hands. Two of which were on the ends of the legs making gripping over unstable surfaces very easy, this Ackrehm knew and apprehended putting them at a clear advantage to his bulky, sometimes clumsy, size. The only real way to survive was to hide, or to detach the group in order to fight them off one putrid creature at a time. Having only a nail for defence, hiding seemed to be the most logical option, but where?

Onward he raced with branches snapping and the sound of slapping from many pairs of hands eagerly following and then suddenly he noticed an overhang of snow was approaching. Spryly as a nymph, Ackrehm dived in and buried himself in the bitter subzero blanket. Snow filled his ears and numbed his face, but still he could hear the enemy racing past, then silence. Were they gone, or just waiting? He could not just burst out straight away, Ackrehm had to give them time to get bored and accept the notion that he was gone, then they would return to their kill and leave him to make good his escape. He waited as long as he could bear the cold, listening all the time, but it got so painful Ackrehm realized that if he was not to move now, then the cold would surely freeze him solid. Expectant that danger had past; he tried as quietly as possible to gain freedom from his icy hideout. Hands out first, clearing the snow from his face so he could see clearly around. Deserted, after several laboured breaths, making sure to be quiet, he arose hunched over and oscillating from the cold, but continuously scanning the surroundings. Carefully he pressed on away from the road and away from the direction the Geflack's had gone in hot pursuit so as not to stumble upon them on their return. Suddenly a blinding pain in his right side, spinning round and grasping at his flank Ackrehm was facing a Geflack reloading his crossbow from forty paces away. Wrenching the dart from his side, Ackrehm's senses took over, he galloped full speed towards the Geflack who was far more concerned with loading his weapon as fast as possible. Looking up, the attacker was greeted with Ackrehm's horns smashing into his face and crushing his head like a brittle walnut against the tree. Stepping back and snorting through both nostrils like an enraged bull, the Geflack's lifeless body slid down the tree. Ackrehm wiped the blood from his face and the mush of brain and hair from his horns. A noise heading his way! Ackrehm froze then realized he had to move, quickly slipping behind some bushy undergrowth; he could watch the approaching Geflack. It crouched over the body of its fallen partner and began sniffing the air, using its club to poke bushes and hissing in distaste at producing nothing. He was getting closer and Ackrehm knew if he was discovered the Geflack could raise the alarm. Remembering he was still holding the nail, Ackrehm drew it back and as the warrior approached within reach, he leapt from the bush driving the nail down with his fist and deep into the Geflacks' eye whilst gripping the back of its head, probing far into its primitive, spiteful brain. With a gurgle and frantic death rattle, Ackrehm threw his victim's body to the floor, placed the bloody nail into his pocket and picked up the Geflacks club.

Like the sky was caving in, Ackrehm was forced to his knees from a blinding blow to the head, falling onto his back as the leader of the Geflacks' stood over him, holding a big cleaver previously hidden on his back. The blow had been so powerful that it was only the Myon's horns that had stopped his head being split like a log. Eyes blurred from the force and his own blood, Ackrehm pushed his body back along the floor, shuffling with his palms as the Geflack walked forward, picking blood off his cleaver and seeing how sticky it was between his fingers with an addicted look that wanted more. Ackrehm shuffled back further still until his back hit a boulder, sitting up against it he wiped his eyes with the backs of his hands trying to clear them, feeling the wound on his head and noticing that one of his horns was hanging off. Split nearly in two by the mighty blow that could so easily have ended his life, but now was he ready to die? The Geflack leader, grinning inanely came forward, giggling and savouring the kill. He came closer and slowly lifted the mighty cleaver, not noticing Ackrehm's hand slipping into his coat pocket and before the leader could deliver the final blow, Ackrehm launched forward forcing the nail deep in to the Geflack's knee. Screaming wildly and trying to escape, the Geflack had lost his cleaver in the deep snow and grasped his leg and turned to limp away to safety, but Ackrehm clasped the creatures sash and would not let go, wiggling the nail uncontrollably so as to cause as much pain as possible. The Geflack pounded down on Ackrehm's head causing him to lose grip from the pain, enabling the leader to slide free. Blindly snatching and grappling, Ackrehm grasped something from the Geflack; it was a weapon, an antler used to place in the palm and punch with, causing serious damage with the spiked protruding horn. This he could use, but first Ackrehm must find his feet and escape for the blood leaking from his crown was not a good sign. From standing and now running he took off, placing the horn weapon in his pocket and then limping, faltering away from the nightmare he had just endured, fear, rage, thirst and pain all coursed through his veins, burning fire like embers and coursing like a shooting star allowing him to run faster and faster until at last he could no longer hear the cries from the Geflack leader, he could no longer hear any attempts to follow after, at last he was alone, encompassed in deafening reticence.

Chapter 4

The cold had frozen droplets of blood to Ackrehm's face and a large, matted, petrified lump in his hair from the sizable head wound. His shirt stuck and ripped off at every step he took, but still he pressed on into the night. The moon shone high in the sky like a rare gem and this light reflected off the white land, lighting the way as good as any bullrush torch. The Myon had to find shelter and warmth if he was to survive the night, but everything was drenched in the frozen cascade that at this point made survival seem redundant. Pressing on and investigating every shadowed area, Ackrehm came across a wooden door, barely visible from the snow that was stuck to it, but on further investigation it was indeed a door. Trying the wooden handle, it broke clean off in Ackrehm's hand. This door must have been closed for many winters, the chances of an enemy or help inside were remote and to scrutinize inside for shelter was a keen idea indeed. Bringing his right leg back he stamped into the door nearest the broken handle in case it was also locked, a loud thud and crack of wood echoed from whatever passage way was inside. He kicked again, then again and then the door shifted open, not much but enough to prove Ackrehm's efforts were not in vain. Leaning his shoulder against the opening side of the door, finding some adequate footholds he pushed, the door creaked and opened some more, now one harder shove and he could squeeze inside. Ackrehm did not want to kick the door in or push it so wide open that he could not shut it again, for not only did he need to keep the wind out as he had no idea how big the room inside was, but he needed to be sure that a keen defence could be made from inside if quintessential.

Squeezing inside and trying to avoid the puncture in his haunch, Ackrehm was able to close the door behind him and disappear in to the darkened burrow that he had uncovered. Feeling deaf blind from the darkness inside and the escape from the cold cyclone outside, he searched the walls, arms outstretched and fingers erect, looking for something to help him find his way. This room had a musty, dry smell of an old ale cellar with cobwebs and dust obstructing, invading his nostrils and mouth like a sand storm, making him sniff and his eyes water from a brewing sneeze. Knocking over what sounded like a wooden pole, Ackrehm bent double to retrieve it, now he had acquired a reaching tool that he could test the darkness in front of him with. Tapping and searching with the wooden stick like a blind beggar, not really sure what he was looking for, but something to light the way would be useful. Tapping into a corner of the room after a near fall over something soft and cumbersome on the floor, Ackrehm noticed a change in the noise the tapping made, this was sort of hollow and stony, a fireplace perhaps? Getting closer and placing the stick under his left arm, he began to feel with his fingers and sure enough it was a fireplace. Dry and depleted with the presence of burnt ruins. At that moment Ackrehm inhaled with supreme hope as if this was a hunting lodge, it was widely understood you always leave some tinder and a flint at the base of the fire, on the off chance a stranded traveller in dire need of warmth, should find the place and the owner was away unable to help. Leaving one hand on the top of the fireplace to act as a guide not to hit his head, Ackrehm crouched down and began feeling around. What luck, this was indeed a hunting lodge or at least the owner was a trapper, there was soft feeling tinder for quick, easy lighting and two hard objects with scrapes and sharp edges, unmistakable as lighting flints. Straight away he made a small mound of the soft lint-like substance and began to chip and strike the flints together creating bright flashes like a meteor shower in the dead of night. It did not take long for a spark to begin an ember, leaning forward and blowing purposefully, deep and direct until smoke and at last a flame began to grow. Even with his eyes and throat stinging from smoke inhalation Ackrehm relaxed slightly, leaning back in relief he sighed and waited for the fire to grow to such an extent that he could finally see the room he had been searching around so blindly.

Feeding the fire with some strips of wood and bark piled neatly at the side of the small, but lifesaving fireplace, Ackrehm began to see his new world, one of simplicity and decadence with nothing more than a small cot of straw and cloth for sleeping, one chair and a small stool with a copper plate on top, plus a crude, weak-looking table for whoever lives or had lived there. Unfortunately, the soft bundle that Ackrehm almost tripped over turned out to be the remains of a dog and it appeared to have been there for quite some time. Fur hanging off and bones visible, but no smell, the rotting had long since passed so the owner of this place must have abandoned it or just never returned. Ackrehm thought back to Therd and how much his companion meant to him, how this poor dog must have waited for his companion to return then just lay down and died by the fire. He did not disturb the peaceful looking dog and just moved around him looking for supplies. Something to eat would be nice, but he would settle for some water or even a cloth to clean the injuries he had sustained.

There was an old cupboard leaning against a wall in the corner which had seemed to have once been attached to the wall due to the holes vertical to the cupboard. So as to examine the contents for any usable substance, Ackrehm knelt on one knee and opened the door. Inside were two broken jars sat in an old and now dry mess, most likely from when the cupboard had fallen. The jars and their contents were lost, but one jar was intact and seemed to contain various vegetables in some sort of pickling liquid. Not a favourite pastime amongst Myon's, but anything would seem like luxury to nothing at this point in time. Also there was a small tobacco box undisturbed and unpolluted by the broken jars spillage. Ackrehm took the box and stood up, opening the lid as he went, discovering a broken charcoal stick, some cotton tightly wrapped around a small stick, and a hip flask that when he lifted, was nearly full. Opening the catch and flipping the lid, a potent smell of surgical alcohol filled his face. Not good for drinking but perfect for cleaning. Taking the one and only undamaged jar of preserves along with the tobacco box and its contents, Ackrehm walked over to the fire and sat cross legged in front to absorb and attain almost a kind of nourishment from its warmth. After sampling some of the food and choking the rigid bitter vegetables down, he put the jar aside and began the arduous and excruciating task of cleaning his wounds with the alcohol. Ripping off some of his undergarments that were, in hindsight, cleaner than anything else he was wearing, Ackrehm removed his coat and shirt to expose his large muscular physique covered with a thick rug of hair. He gently tested the damage to his side from the Geflack's dart with his fingers, picking off some dried blood and making sure in his mind he could stand the pain of cleaning it. Whether he could stand it or not, infection was a frightening notion and cleansing the wound was the only option. Pouring a few spurts of the alcohol onto the torn cloth, he passed it from his right hand to his left so as to be able to smother his injury completely. Taking a deep breath and gritting his teeth, Ackrehm pushed the cloth onto his side, trembling in agony at first and then breathing rapidly through tightly clamped teeth. The pain escalated quickly like cold feet being plunged into a hot bath; then as quickly as it rose, the pain dissipated and Ackrehm hunched, double breathing deeper and slower. Sweat beads crowded his brow and trickled down to the tip of his nose before he irritably wiped them away with the back of his forearm. Waiting for a moment for his head to clear and his breathing to at last return to normal, Ackrehm inspected the carving in his head. Disaster, his left horn was barely attached, cut almost to his skull. For a Myon this was worse than death, their horns were a source of great pride and power and to lose one would make him only half a male. Sometimes a broken horn did grow back, but often when reaching adulthood, they would only grow back thinner and weaker than before at best. Feeling around his misfortune, Ackrehm grew more and more angry. Jumping to his feet and storming outside wearing nothing but his loin cloth, prizing the door open and dropping to his knees in the raging snow storm that enslaved the forest, he began to scoop up snow using both hands and packing it tightly against his head wound, more and more he piled on and compressed down. Struggling to breathe in the cold, bitter wind, sleet and hail stinging his growing blue body, Ackrehm stood upright, his eyes tumid from the blizzard and every muscle tensed to the point of explosion. He pushed away the snow covering his head with both hands, then after testing the area was securely numb from the cold with a few sharp pokes from his finger, he grasped the horn with his right hand and strained in fury and anguish breaking the horn from its cut off point. The loud crack like summer lightning rang in his frozen ears and standing there; looking at his severed manhood he wept and then turned, carrying his horn, staggering back into his private hideout, shivering as he went with heavy footsteps like the moon was resting on his shoulders. Stepping inside and leaning against the door, to seal himself and his pride away from the harshness of this boorish and abominable exterior, his mind began to sink into a frozen sullenness.

Chapter 5
The Geflacks

The Geflack leader of a large band of marauding heathens, was powerful and merciless amongst his clan, but today Kadamlic had been smited by a lone Myon and was drooling with rage-filled vengeance in his black little heart. He stumbled through the snow, back to the path that he and four others had so hastily departed from, wincing every time he put weight on the leg previously injured after such a sure possibility of slaying an adult Myon and becoming a hero. Out of breath and running from behind were Kadamlic's two surviving soldiers, he hissed for assistance and they at once came to his aid.

Kadamlic shouted, "Where were you two cowards when he attacked me from behind?"

The two Geflack solders said nothing for fear of angering him more and just took an arm each, draping it over their shoulders and helping Kadamilc walk back to the path.

"That Myon will curse the day it dropped from its mother's crouch, killing two of my best and then attacking me from behind, what insult!"

Kadamlic knew not only was he pleased to see his other two men to help him walk, but he also knew that he had to pretend he was ambushed by a coward rather than caught off guard when he had the upper hand. Such truths could sanction distrust amongst his clan and that would prove no value for future domination.

Returning to the road, many of the Geflacks had begun returning meat back to their camp and the wagon had been completely taken to pieces. Anything useful had been taken and only the bare scraps remained, but even those had been sifted through and a fire had been set to cook up some of the horse meat there and then. Several were crouching round a small fire with meat being turned on a spit over the flames. One of the Geflacks' noticed Kadamlic being carried back and stood up and away from the fire knowing the mood that Kadamlic would be in, it was best not to be seen resting and enjoying a good feed.

The closer they got, more and more of the Geflacks' stood and backed away from the fire, the one that still sat who had his back to the returning three was more interested in the meat he was trying to force into an already full mouth. Right behind the seated Geflack now, Kadamlic raised his good leg and kicked the seated scavenger in the back of the neck sending him flying onto the fire. Set ablaze and rolling around screeching and wailing, the dregs saw fit not to try and aid the enflamed dupe, for if their leader had seen fit to end him then that was what had to happen, interference would most certainly meet with the same punishment or much, much worse.

"Had your fill have you bastard?! You stand when I approach!" Kadamilc bellowed.

The smell of burning flesh protruded like an arrow in the chest, tickling and choking the others, making them step back further away from their vexed leader. Kadamlic pushed away his two supports and sat where the charred Geflack had previously enjoyed his meal, reaching down for the same strips of meat, grasping one length and tearing at it whilst still staring daggers at his band.

"Clean away that insolent piece of dung and get all the rest back to camp."

Pointing at the smallest Geflack of all, then pointing back to his injured knee he spat his commands. "Fix this or feel my blade, I won't become as lame as the rest of you, now MOVE!"

Spitting chunks of cooked flesh and saliva as he barked his orders, the others exploded into action like mice disturbed by a candle light. Everyone gathered their weapons and packs of supplies together then scurried off into the darkness. Still finishing his meal and having his leg attended, Kadamlic was in awe of the camp flames, eyes glistening like black fire opals made silent vows, vows to wipe this Myon from the face of the land, to make his death decidedly slow and caustic. Tonight he would sacrifice one of their young in offering to Doeithis, the Geflack goddess of retribution, she would make his hands faster and his mind keener than the Myon's, her appeased, there was nothing to stop him or stand in his way.

Breaking the silence, a thundering beast carrying a large basket strapped to his back appeared from the darkness. This colossus was a slave to the Geflacks, once a peaceful mountain dweller, the simple minded 'Oaf' had been captured and tortured into imprisonment, turned into an animal worthy of only kitchen scraps and had become Kadamlic's own personal steed. Bare footed, wearing only a kilt and a huge iron mask bound to the Oaf's head he slowed and came to rest at the side of Kadamlic. He pointed to the ground and the oaf obeyed bending until his body was low enough for the Geflack leader to climb on, being aided by his assistant. Banging the huge iron mask, the oaf rose to standing, proud and mighty he stood like a stallion in heat he awaited his orders.

"Homeward!"

And with that the oaf took off back into the darkness from whence it came, bounding leviathan strides with its master, Kadamlic, leader of the Geflacks, standing arrogantly on his back feeling mighty and at last back in command heading home to plan his revenge.

Chapter 6
Prophecy

The Geflack kingdom was indeed mighty, with centuries positioned for supreme protection against all who would dare to venture in. The air thick with the smell of decay and all around was silence, not even the birds sang here, in the place where death was apparent and rampant.

Morning had created a solemn emptiness where the creatures slept in their rancid little holes like huge rodents. The only real structures were of Kadamlic's quarters which stood above ground and housed himself and only the select few of his servants and slaves. This above ground fortress was impenetrable; the only access was from a huge entrance underground leading to chased tunnels, winding and black, passing through dwellings and dungeons of the troops at Kadamlic's appropriation. Great warriors of his clan were permitted to enter only on his request whilst planning the day's raids and slaughter. Kadamlic was the only Geflack still conscious; he was troubled greatly by the absence of the Myon. Lying on his animal skin mound and fixated on his collection of weapons mounted on the walls, he concocted many different scenarios in his head of what was to be done with the Myon. Most ended with Kadamlic torturing him in the most horrific fashions, leaving him maimed and mutilated beyond recognition and repair. Stopping only to allow the Myon to regain consciousness and begin the hideous routine all over again. But time was required for his leg to heal; it would not be a leader's wisdom to rush straight out into the wilderness possibly for many days with a fresh injury and not fighting fit, for the Myon would surely triumph. He must not seem weak and forgiving in the eyes of the other Geflacks', he must continue to rule with a rod of iron, not giving any ambiguity that he alone was in command, for mutiny was common amongst Geflack communities, new rulers were frequent and did not last long if they allowed affronts to go unpunished.

After what seemed like an eternity, Kadamlic rose from his trance to check the condition of his wound. It was fresh and deep, but clean and well dressed. Healing should be prompt if he made sure the slaves took care of it. Throwing a copper cup against his door creating a loud din, something outside sprang into action and the door flew open.

"Yes sir?" the guard enquired.

Kadamlic replied, "Awaken my idle consult I want to talk with him, oh and get me some water before you feel my rage!"

With that the guard quickly exited and went about the tasks of which he had been instructed for it was astute to do as you were told working directly for Kadamlic himself. Bodies were of a constant obstruction in the halls of his domain and insolence was extinguished directly and swiftly. Soon after, a hunched and aged Geflack slowly entered Kadamlic's chamber. Gently clicking the wooden floor boards as he went with his staff and wearing a hood of black and a beard of grey. This was the high priest and most trusted of all the Geflack community, rulers came and went, but Himleigh would stay until the end of his days, to serve and advise, for few knew the ways of the Geflack people more intuitively than Himleigh. Kadamlic observed the old consorts every move from his seat of power, never lifting his head Himleigh seemed to drift across the room as if in a realm of his own, untouched and unafraid of his leaders' watchful and intrusive gaze. Reaching a table at the far end of the room, Himleigh pulled back his hood to reveal an aged and troubled brow, skin turned white with age and wrinkled like an old leather saddle bag, but shining so brightly was his silver eye. Lost in battle in his younger years, this eye was a frightening sight to most of the tribe, for it is said to have the power to look deep in to your soul and read ones most secret desires.

"You get slower by the day old one."

"Rushing in will only cause one to falter... My king."

"If that was an insult I will have you skinned!"

"I come simply to advise sire, nothing more."

Kadamlic knew this was a flippant remark on how he became to be injured, but a warning was to suffice. Not in his wildest dreams would he or his troops dare harm such a trusted and feared individual as Himleigh, plus his advice was not only required, but it was very much respected. Himleigh reached into his cloak and produced a young Geflack. It was wrapped in a cloth and sleeping soundly; cradled by the old consort and rocked gently it began to stir. Himleigh lifted the infant high in to the air and closed his eyes mouthing silent prayers.

"For our goddess, Doeithis." Himleigh said.

And with that he clasped the young by its leg and swung with all his might allowing its head to collide with the corner of the table, killing it instantly. He laid the limp body onto the table and proceeded to examine the sizable head wound, poking a long bony finger inside and feeling around. It is said that a sacrifice such as this to the goddess of vengeance will not only make the Geflack's retribution swift and unmerciful, but the method in which this should be undertaken can be read in the brains of the young.

Stepping away from the table and walking over to his ever observant king, Himleigh wiped his fingers clean on his cloak, head bowed in thought.

"It seems you have quite a problem. The goddess thinks this fight is lost, the Myon is seen to bring us down from within."

"Rubbish, you're just scared, that's not what she said. I offer her the death of a young and she will grant me what I ask!"

"Sire, she has spoken to me through this death, if you seek the Myon, we are all to end."

"Then I will offer her a thousand dead young, whatever it takes! I want this bastard's skin hanging from my walls, I want to taste his heart and feel its last beat in my hand.

"As you wish sire, I shall retire now my consumption grows, I need my herbs."

"Very well, have someone clean these lies off my table and don't pant a word of this to anyone!"

Slowly Himleigh regressed and left the king alone with his cogitation. Kadamlic's head was on fire with rage, confusion and panic. If he ignored the reading, then bad luck was sure to follow, but it is written in the Geflack law, that ignominy and dishonour must be dealt with swiftly and without amnesty. Head spinning with unanswered questions he fell back onto his soft animal skins and allowed himself to drift off in to deeply troubled and opaque stupor.

Chapter 7

Himleigh wandered reluctantly back to his dwellings, along dirt tunnels he staggered on to the most secluded part of the dominion, reserved for him and him alone. The respect held for Himleigh was the most highly ever bestowed upon a single personage and he knew it. A cunningly placed word from him could achieve the most impressive results, even going so far as to cause a revolt and knock the so called monarch from his mighty indomitable perch. As he entered his chamber, two standing guards tilted their helmets in adoration of their elder and stood aside allowing him to enter. As the door closed behind him, Hemleigh exhaled acutely and hung his cloak on a hook emanating from the rear of the door.

"Fool!"

Knowing the intentions of his king and how wrong they were was hard to swallow, but there is not a Geflack in the realm that would not have to act in the same way. Reprisal is their way of life, but it is possible that the soul reason Himleigh has lived so long and is so unanimously respected is due to the fact he abandoned these primal urges long ago giving way to a more enlightened and intellectual commitments.

Kadamlic limped about his chamber, the prophecy told by Himleigh weighing heavy on his mind. There must be a way to seek revenge without being seen to directly ignore a highly respected consult and not to mention the bad fortune that could befall him by turning his back on the goddess, Doeithis. Lighting a candle and carrying it to the window, he contemplated an idea. What if he were to summon a death squad? It had been many years since the Geflacks' sought outside help, but these hired warriors could be seen to be acting alone away from his command. Also if ever found out, he could deny any allegations to such plotting and have the accusers burned alive taking their secrets to the grave.

"GUARD!" shouted Kadamlic.

The clanging of metal and rushed footsteps grew louder outside the door until it slowly creaked open. A Geflack in full battle dress holding a large spear peered around the door.

Guard: "Sire?"

"Send for my scouts, the two fastest runners we have and have them here at once!"

"Right away sire."

Pelting down the corridor away from the king's quarters, the guard clipped every wall and scraped his spear off the ceiling, spraying scratching dust into his eyes. Round a bend to the left, then another he reached the stone staircase. Darkened and deep it went, to the realm of the Geflacks. Down he went, twisting and turning to fit his laden body, until at last he hit dirt and was at the entrance to one of the many rabbit-like burrows that held the nest of workers and solders. Turning right in to darkness, his giant eyes reflected every flicker from the sparsely placed wall lanterns, mud squelched under his feet like hands and his breathing became heavy and laboured. Further he went until he came to a very thin entrance that bore many small wooden doors inside. This was the soldiers' section; it housed not only the foot soldiers and archers, but the scouts.

Turning sideways to slide in the entrance, he went in and walked along, every door had a carving on to show what skill the Geflack inside had; an arrow for archer, a sword for heavy weapons, a spear for a piker, a club for light attackers and many different weapons carved for all round scrappers. The doors stopped and the tunnel continued, this was where the guard was to find the scouts. At last several doors all on one side bore the marks of the scout, a huge eye with a dagger as a pupil. He stopped at the first door and with a spear clasped hand he hit twice. Slowly it opened and a tiny muscular Geflack opened and stood showered in almost total darkness, looking the guard up and down he spoke with a rasping scratchy voice.

"Ahhhh, the kings very own guard if I'm not mistaken."

"Raith, you're the fastest scout we have, gather your things and choose an accomplice, the king demands your presence."

Turning, the guard bounded off down the tunnel and Raith stepped out calling after him.

"But what for?"

Raith thought the guard was either deaf or more likely didn't know, either way he must move quickly as a chance for combat might be near and certainly should not be missed. He pulled a large leather bag from under his wooden frame bunk and rummaged through it, pulling out his kilt and quickly wrapped it around his waist. Then he removed a hemp waistcoat and slid into it, fastening the front with an iron buckle. He strapped a dagger to his inner left calf and threw a small satchel over his head, bringing it to rest by his side. Raith kicked the half empty bag back under his bunk and raced for the door pulling it closed behind him. Orders were to bring an accomplice which he did not like one bit, Raith worked alone for stealth and furtiveness, bringing an accomplice was foreign to his methods, but orders were orders. He stood outside his closed door and contemplated a worthy comrade, turning and slowly walking past the scouts' rooms his eyes burned in past the wooden frames and envisaged the Geflack inside, weighting up their skills and psyches. The first den was retained by Slot; he was fat and had given himself away far too often to be of any use in a silent faction. Moving on and looking at doors, Raith plagued his intuition for the perfect partner and suddenly it came to him. Fifth door along, Cleave! He was the most logical choice, fast, small and as shapely and guileful as his name suggested. Gunning along to hide five, Raith raised his hand to rap on the door when it drew quickly inwards and standing in the wake was Cleave.

"You stalk these halls like an Oaf." he said with a brazen grin showing fangs filed sharp and lips as black as pitch.

"Never mind your cheek, get your things, we are to report to Kadamlic for a mission."

"Both of us?"

"It would seem so; I was instructed to pick an accomplice, but as the best was busy you will have to do, for the moment anyway."

They both smiled and Cleave retreated into his hovel returning moments later in a long cloak that not only obscured his face, but the collection of throwing blades strapped to his chest and around his waist. Together they turned and headed with gait and conjecture to present themselves before the King of the Geflacks and impute their mission.

Chapter 8
Planning

Kadamlic awaited the arrival of his scouts whilst he supped on a stone goblet of the dead young Geflack's blood. It was a treat afforded only by the king after such readings. The blood is drained into a container and stirred briskly to remove any clots; these are later dried and salted for royal nutritional morsels, a solemn knock rang from his door causing him to raise one eyebrow. "Enter."

Raith entered and Cleave followed, they stopped after several steps into the room and stood side by side both bowing their heads in unison then they poised erect.

"Well now, I'm sure you are both well aware of a rather troublesome encounter yesterday evening and how I sustained a minor injury but a major insult at the hands of a filthy Myon!" The spite was evident in Kadamlic's speech, spitting as he spoke and clasping the goblet with all his might causing his knuckles to turn white. "I have summoned you both here for a covert siege upon this bastard and it is to be kept strictly between we three, is that clear?"

"Clear!" they answered together.

"Good, good. Well I charge you both to seek out some hired meat for this mission. I don't want the spilling of any more of our precious Geflack blood, six including you both should be plenty to take this animal down, after all, I wounded him myself before he turned and ran off like a cowardly Gump into the forest. I will offer one thousand troy of gems to bring him back alive. The payment will be waiting on your return."

Raith and Cleave knew very well that there was no way their king would honour such a sizable debt and they were the ones whose lives would be in jeopardy should this errand be successful and payment was sought. This was indeed a problem for them both, deny their king and be tortured to death or complete the task and face the need for desertion to survive.

"Fully understood sire, are we to assist the hired hunters in this task?" asked Raith.

"No, I think it better for you to observe from a distance, after all that's what you're good at, just make sure this shit is brought to me alive, here's a purse to wet their appetites."

"Yes, master."

Kadamlic tossed a small cloth bag that jingled with metal as it landed at their feet, Raith and Cleave both tilted their heads in sequence again and turned for the door, Cleave scooping up the purse as they went; just as Raith's hand touched the lever to exit, Kadamlic added an even weightier burden to this already ample problematic task.

"Oh, and one more thing, if you fail, you might as well join the Myon in hiding and anticipate the pain I will put you through with my branding irons. That will be all, you leave immediately."

Leaving Kadamlic grinning inanely, Raith and Cleave stood outside the door looking at each other in silent agreement, understanding that they were indeed on a task with such astringency that it may very well be their final moments that are beginning to unfold.

Chapter 9
Ackrehm

Three of the most abased days in all his life had passed since the death of Therd and the loss of his most sacred components. Animosity and compunction consumed him in a strangle hold as fierce and unrelenting as an avalanche. The pain of his wounds only exaggerated complete and utter relinquishment of sanity.

Barely moving from the fire, he lay on one side transfixed by the flames, wondering and deliberating how he had been wronged and how he was now worthless in the eyes of the Myons'. Hunger and injury had drained his energy so completely that even sitting up strained his muscles, but as he did so, his gaze cruised across the floor to the heap that once was a dog, loyal and fearless as most were in these lands; this creature had accepted his fate and awaited the eternal rest that was to follow. Was this to be his fate also, scorned and battered, dying alone and ashamed in a forgotten hollow? All these ideas flooded the banks of his psyche and laid seeds of doubt that abandonment was not the correct choice. After all, surely he was more driven and directed than this poor dog. Ackrehm used his arm to raise himself to a seated position, to further his view of the mound of bones and skin, this was not to be him, this was not to be the resting place of a Myon!

Pushing himself to his feet Ackrehm stumbled and stooped to one knee. Holding his side and pushing off his leg he stood again, hunched but aware that the time for survival was like the sands of a timer and were rapidly absconding.

Ackrehm staggered out of his room and down the tight passageway to the door, leaning against the wall as he went. Dust trickled down his shoulder and flicked into his face as he scraped along, the need to get outside was intoxicating as he slumped against the door, his shell from the world needed to be broken and he pulled with all his might at the loop of cord that acted as a handle from the inside. Steadily it opened with a dry scratching noise and light began to pour in, illuminating his darkened world. The air was chilled, but fresh as he stepped into the morning snow crunching underfoot and placid bird songs penetrated the silence from the treetops. He moved out into the open and surveyed his surroundings, for the first time visible unlike in the storm he had endured before. Having no idea of how far he had travelled in his injured state it was imperative he was secluded and out of danger's grasp, for in his still weakened state he could surely not defend himself.

This place was beautiful, untouched and unspoiled by clans or tribes, the rays of light pierced through branches and created a calmness and welcoming sensation he had longed to feel throughout his depression. Moving forward he could hear the trickling of a small stream fuelled by melting ice and snow causing him to lick his dry tongue against the roof of his mouth. Onward he went to the source and crouched by the stream's bank, wincing from his side he leant forward and let the cool current fill his mouth and sooth his dry, cracked lips. Ackrehm supped the energy from the drift, swirling liquid around his mouth then gulping like a tired horse. Lightly rejuvenated he sat back on a rock as droplets fell from his furry chin onto his chest, icy as they trickled down and bringing life to his skin.

Splashing caught his attention further on down and he poised and extended his gaze to see what it was, a fish! What luck this stream could not only provide fresh, thirst quenching aqua, but perhaps a chance to feed. Still holding his side, Ackrehm got to his feet and crept over to the noise, sure enough there were small fish congregating in the currents and holding their own looking for insects; too weak to make a snatch, Ackrehm started to collect rocks from the water's edge and build a small dam. Slowly it grew and he had built an area for the water and its companions to flow into then filter out leaving the fish, shallow and unable to escape. After he built the trap he left it alone in hope that upon his return, the meal would be waiting. A further surveillance of his new if only temporary home was in order and off he walked, slowly looking from side to side, up and down. Trying to memorize every tree and rock placement, every hill and bush and to see what else this area had to offer. Tracks from fowl and rodent littered the fresh fallen snow all along the river where creatures had come to indulge themselves, so being a competent trapper, Ackrehm was indeed smiling on the inside, knowing where to place snares was his vocation and he was sure this was a place that had not been farmed of wildlife for quite some time. The possibility of the critters neophobia was indeed a challenge but one he relished and sufficient disguise of these traps would be just the answer.

Chapter 10
Raith and Cleave

The pair trudged slowly through the spiteful rain, shielding their big black eyes with hoods and hands. Moving in the paths of trees to avoid most of the brutal weather; neither needed to exchange conversation and both were laden with the arduous task befallen them. The mud squelched under their palms, oozing between their lower fingers, being as thick as their minds were with thought and questions, finally after nearly a night's worth of walking in silence Cleave could restrain from airing his thoughts no longer.

"You're a wonderful conservationist."

"And you talk too much."

Raith, who was slightly ahead in their party of two, glanced over his shoulder with a sinister grin making Cleave smile wryly. "If we are to hire thugs we will need protection."

"Exactly, who is to trust a mercenary not to shiv you in the neck when they feel like it?"

"Kadamlic… Well the king has spoken of a new mode of transport he fancies, the oaf is too stupid and he wants more of a 'warhorse'."

"As walking would be too much for him!" said Cleave.

"Watch your tone Geflack, we may share opinions on our liege you and I, but these thoughts should not be put to voice… Not yet anyway."

Cleave irritated by Raith's correction grunted in acknowledgement and kept moving. The rain was dying down now to a fine spray, soaking cloak and skin to the bone, a toppled tree ahead provided an adequate shelter from the elements and a place to gather strength and warmth.

Raith said, "In here."

Both Geflacks moved into the hollow of the uprooted tree, the mud and earth clung to the roots like a clay roof and kept the pair dry enough to continue their thoughts without elemental interruption.

"So, this new "warhorse", what's it to do with our task?" asked Cleave

"Say we find a beast and get it to join us, or more protect us. Then not only serving us in our mission, I'm sure the King would like to keep it after, as a gift, that and the Myon".

"Pretty clever, can't hurt to have extras for… what's the word for such an 'insistent' monarch?"

"Well said, Cleave. Just convincing the bastard to join will be the next challenge, but Cyclops' are easily bribed."

"Cyclops? Troll shit!"

"Knew you'd be pleased."

Raith and Cleave both sat with their knees up to their chests, cocooned in their cloaks and still in the darkness. It was only the pungent light shining from the moon that betrayed their position, sparkling off their black eyes and dancing under their hoods. Cleave began to drowse and doze whilst Raith sat in thought. Raith had requisitioned more of his own coin before leaving the Geflack's Kingdom for further bribing the help, but did he have enough? Well he really only needed to pay the Cyclops, the others could go spit after the job was done. This thought made him smile again and the sight spoke of a true menace, he was indeed a picture of Geflack and a credit to all their manipulative and wicked kind.

After two more rainless hours, the sun began to rise. Spilling over the forest floor like the oil shimmering on a blacksmith's water trough. It reached like talons through the water blushed leaves and the first bird song could be heard. Both the scouts looked at each other and again unconsciously agreed it was time to move. Geflacks must stick to the shadows and ensure they are never seen; they liked surprise and they meant to keep to it. Cleave had found his bearings in the respite and knew of the town close by. Neeson was a small but busy crossroads town with merchants meeting to discuss prices and barter through most of the year. Everything could be bought or sold in Neeson and this is probably why the Cyclops was rumoured to be skulking close by. Kadamlic had boasted how he would travel to Neeson and capture the beast for his personal chariot, only there was always a more pressing issue at hand. Raith despised his incessant boasting and remedial actions; if anything else with him persuading the Cyclops to join would certainly allow the hordes to see that he was more suited to be king than Kadamlic. Ideas of grandeur polluted his brain and set wicked cogs turning, after all when this was over why indeed could he not rule? He was more of a Geflack than Kadamlic would ever be! Still there was plenty of time for that, appeasing Kadamlic was required at present and the death of the Myon would be his own personal victory and would be on the lips of all the Geflacks.

Chapter 11

Raith and Cleave moved like mice through the undergrowth and bushes, silent as disease they spread until, at last, hammering could be heard. The blacksmiths were early risers, shoeing horses for the guests and merchants staying at the Neeson tavern. They were busy all hours of the day and sometimes night in the summer months so the scouts knew they were close. Moving slightly further they could see a main road leading into the township at the bottom of their slope; burrowed in to the hill and brush like ticks on a hound they observed the area undetected.

Raith made a click with his tongue to get Cleave's attention and then motioned with his head over to the far side of the road. Cleave noticed right away what Raith had seen, broken and twisted branches at the side of the road, some cloth in the same area hanging from the brambles and the stain of blood turned brown on the edge of the cobbles. Passers-by would hardly notice the damage as something had made an attempt to disguise the path, if they had noticed they would think it the scene of an old accident. An upended cart and a merchants wares could have spilled due to a broken cart wheel. The scouts had a feeling this was more than it appeared; this was where the Cyclops would hunt, waiting in seclusion and watching, patiently scrutinizing the passers until the light was low, the danger was minimal and the pickings were fruitful.

The Geflacks eyed the area for some further moments, looking for signs of movement, but nothing. They would have to wait and find cover, hidden from the world and more importantly the Cyclops, for these beasts were known to eat any flesh they desired and Geflacks' although fast and nimble were no match for a determined Cyclops, especially in such meagre numbers. So higher up the hill they skulked, ever watching behind and scanning around for beings that could betray their position. They found a nice, low hanging tree that spread wide and was bushy to obscure themselves from the onlookers in, but allow freedom of sight out. Perched off the wet grasses and in a light morning breeze they began to dry in clothes and in mind, formulating silent plans alone until one was suitable enough to share.

Cleave of course was the first to speak. "Should we not just move in dark to where the Cyclops could be, find him and offer coin?"

"If you surprise a Cyclops you best make sure he's fed and watered, unless you are feeling slightly suicidal?"

"Then we wait for some poor bastard to be taken, after the commotion we move in and offer our deal."

"Better and if we are rejected?" asked Raith

"Then the beast will be tired and when he sleeps I will take his eye for my own keeping."

"A finer plan and Geflack there is none. Now we wait… And in silence."

Cleave nodded and turned back to the ambush site, all eight hands of the pair were secured and poised ready to fire them out of sight and into cover should the need arise, but for now calm blanketed their world.

Time was passing slowly along with a multitude of traders, races and creatures; at one point Cleave thought he saw a Richten, an amphibious type creature that could walk upright and could swim for fathoms on one single breath, but they were too far from the sea for this race so his eyes must have fooled him. The scouts occasionally shared scraps of food taken with them; dried fish and slithers of rancid meat like true carrion to tide them over after such a trek and now the waiting grew long. Soon the light grew dim and carts became fewer and sparser in their passing, bullrush torches and oil lanterns were being lit and the Geflacks could relax more for obscurity became easier now, night truly was their friend and they welcomed it. From the veritable stampede of life the road was now trickling along like a dying stream, carts took even longer to approach and they could be heard from quite a distance, this was such an obviously good hunting ground for a Cyclops, it was no surprise he was here.

Chapter 12
The Cyclops

Deep into dark after an age of nothingness came a creaking, the repetitive and mundane noise of old wooden wheels on stone, sounded clear over the area and began to grow closer; gently placed hooves were heard in sporadic unison suggesting this was a small cart being pulled by a tired pony and undoubtedly exhausted traveller from the hour.

Raith sniffed rather abruptly to gain Cleaves attention and eyed the direction of sound; he spoke in a whisper, smiling and poised. "Bait."

Closer and closer came the noise, a little light could be seen rocking frantically and flickering from the branches and leaves obscuring its beams, then a step was heard, not from the trader, this was much much closer and from a large heavy gate. Wind tickled rustling of leaves concealed the beast and silence reigned once more apart from the eerie echo of the cart moving closer. The Cyclops was here, it had heard the lone dinner bell of a cart in the night and had come sniffing for a feast.

Smoking a straw-thin and nicotine stained pipe, an elderly elf merchant was propelling along at a meagre rate, obviously in no hurry to reach his destination. The pony on point was stout and round like a keg with legs, more pet than workman's tool; it had been spoilt over the years not rushed or spurned, but cared for and made companion by her master. Slowly as he puffed she pulled, drearily placing one hoof in front of the other with her head bobbing up and down like a fisherman's float in a stream as calm as this night.

Deep within a hut-sized bush danger lurked in the form of a dinner bowl sized eye. Yellow and sliced with red blood vessels the unblinking eye fixated on the merchant and his pony, staring like a lover at a cheating spouse, it watched as the cart drew closer, patiently it waited and closer drew its target of affections. Silently, two giant, hairless, three fingered paws rested a pace in front of the eye showing how large this beast truly was. Its veins pulsated in its swollen scar-riddled forearms and even the leather wrist binds looked like twine around a baking loaf. As the cart creaked onward, a meagre twenty paces and closing, the griffin-like paws pushed fingers into the earth for purchase and leverage so it could explode into motion in a single blink of its moon-like eye.

Blissfully unaware, the elf merchant was enjoying his smoke and uncommonly mild, cool evening breeze, transfixed in thought of the past and briefly re-joining reality with a swish of the pony's tail before drifting off again, age and the hour had created the merchant's equilibrium from which he bathed, ignorance truly was bliss for the elf.

Like seeing lightning flashes before hearing the thunder, the merchant saw something that resembled a pale blue, hairless bear bursting out of the forest before hearing it. Frozen in fright and awe he had not motivation to spur on his pony, but yet sit and observe his short lived fate the Cyclops had written for him. Ploughing into the pony with arms spread the Cyclops constricted the pony's neck and stood to his full height lifting her front hooves off the floor, the clasp as a tourniquet on her throat cutting off her air along with their escape. Frantically her front hooves paddled and cycled, running on air, screaming desperation along with her whinny's and rapid eye movement. The Cyclops clasped his own forearm for leverage and with a ravenous smile shook the pony, pulling in with his arms and leaning forward with his mighty chest in an attempt to break her neck. Seconds passed like an eternity for the merchant and only after several loud snaps of equine vertebrae did the Cyclops release his hold on the pony and likewise the hypnotic retention he had over the merchant.

As the merchant found his lungs again and started to breathe, the Cyclops did a quick scout around with his enormous eye for any supporters to the merchant. Satisfied they were alone, the Cyclops puffed out his chest, bared his tombstone-like teeth and approached the merchant, bleaching him in shadow like a lunar eclipse as the Cyclops was still just taller than the merchant even though he was still sat aloft on his cart.

The merchant choked out a word on the smoke he had been clutching too along with faint hope and both left him in a trickled, laboured stammer fearing never to return. "Ssssppare me."

The merchant, trembling and fearful as he spoke; the Cyclops grinned again in a failed attempt to look friendly, as if it was even possible after what he had done to the pony, the moon making his blood spattered face look like it was blessed in fat black tears.

The Cyclops quickly grasped the merchant's feet in his right paw and hauled him into the air and upside down. The merchant swung from side to side like a child's pendulum toy, thrashing his arms to remove his cloak from his face and to swat at the Cyclops in an effort to break free. The Cyclops began to chuckle and with his left paw he prodded the old elf merchant encouraging him to swing further and this only made him thrash more; fuelling the Cyclops's amusement, but as the merchant drew a large breath to let out a scream for help, the Cyclops quickly used his left hand to secure the merchant's head between its mighty fingers and with a sharp pull of both arms, the merchant's neck and back snapped. The Cyclops held him upside down for a second longer, bringing him in for closer inspection from his huge eye, looking for signs of life where there were none. Satisfied the old elf was dead; he tossed his limp corpse in to the back of his own cart and moved back to the pony. Its twitching had stopped and it lay, tongue out, on the road, its neck distorted like an aged tree branch and empty eyes staring up at the sky again leading its master to the heavens compliments of their Cyclops encounter.

The beast bent double and scooped up the pony, carrying it over to the cart with his head and neck dangling like a droughted flower in the night he placed its body on the cart and tucked the head in on top of its master like he had done this a hundred times before, the Cyclops stood at the front of the cart rubbing his palms together and making a sound like sandpaper he then clasped the shafts of the cart and like an oversized wheelbarrow, the Cyclops pushed his new found possessions back through the bushes from where he had so abruptly emerged, after the cart was out of sight, the Cyclops returned to the scene of the crime, only to cover his tracks with branches and bushes he had seemingly already prepared, taking time to check and admire his work he then turned back to the cart and continued to push it away, out of sight and soon out of ear shot of the Geflacks. They had watched on in silence, observing the whole mugging and in true Geflack style they were suitably unmoved.

"He's a big one hey, to kill a pony with his bare hands like that," said Cleave.

"Like a hammer, strong and blunt, but only truly effective if controlled by a skilled hand. We will wait till it's had a feed and time to doze off before we move in and make ourselves known," replied Raith.

"Agreed."

Agreed? Raith thought, he had not made a suggestion, it was an instruction. The sooner Cleave stopped seeing them as equals the better, he thought, Raith had already decided he would not share the spoils of this successful mission, Cleave would have to go, but not until his fulfilled his usefulness.

Chapter 13

An iridescent icy mist had swamped the bushes making the Cyclops' tracks disappear like rain in a stream. Raith and Cleave pressed forward, all hands feeling outward, gently searching for twists and turns, branches and other trips so as to keep noise to a minimum. Cleave thought he was as silent as a snowflake, but Raith would have disagreed, the occasional leaf crunching under hand echoed like thunder in Raith's ears. He held back slightly letting Cleave take point. Should there be a sudden danger, Cleave would be the topic of its focus first leaving Raith time to escape or hide.

Cleave stopped suddenly; a smell had pierced his nostrils like an arrow to the head, a mixture of body odour and rat urine that was typical of a Cyclops infected the mist and betrayed his whereabouts. Raith snuck alongside him and together they heard the rhythmic din of repetitive snores from a slumbering beast. Slowly Raith and Cleave filtered through the bushes and came to the germinating growth of light from a camp fire, the snores continuing and signified to the Geflacks that their presence had not thus far been detected so they could continue to check the area.

Raith moved stealthily around the clearing ever keeping one eye on the gigantic slumbering mound that was the Cyclops's back facing the fire, torn clothing and charred meat strewn on the floor like the morning after a spring festival, the

Cyclops looked to have had his fill of the merchant and his pony, cooked and consumed right away, the remains spoke of a savage meal that had just taken place. The repetitive breathing continued and the Geflacks moved, but not once did Raith's eyes leave the Cyclops' back. Cleave, on the other hand, was becoming content of the sleeping giant and became brazen and inquisitive, searching for useful wears and coin Cleave became bolder still, moving closer and indeed louder towards the Cyclops. Rummaging without care and unawares the breathing had changed; hastened after a particularly loud sniff from Cleave. This detail had not gone unnoticed by Raith and he backed to the edge of the clearing, observing Cleave and the Cyclops, awaiting what he felt would be an 'AWAKENING' moment for both concerned.

Under Raith's unsung supervision, Cleave moved closer to the warm glow of the flames, its heat emanated and serenaded, drawing him closer like a moth to a candle. The light engulfed his big nocturnal eyes and momentarily rendered the Cyclops to be one with the shadows, but he did not care. Feeling the warmth he moved in closer holding out his upper hands so they might tingle with returning blood after the days and weeks of cold.

The Cyclops' eye opened, its pupil became small and its nostrils flickered. He knew he had a visitor and he creased a slight grin over his scar filled face. Continuing the sleeping façade, he lay with his back to the fire, soaking in the smell of rain evaporating from the wet clothes of his new guest, but Cleave felt in awe of the flame and warmth, moving almost on top of it for maximum heat he peeked over at the sleeping beast, still sleeping he thought and no sign of danger. Raith looked on and thought how the Cyclops could prove himself useful much sooner than expected.

Cleave with arms outstretched, closed his eyes to bask in the ambiance of the warm glow on his tired face and before he could even open his eyes, Cleave was hoisted into the air by his arms. Trapped in the vice-like grip of the Cyclops' mighty paws, Cleave sharply kicked his legs but to no avail, they were too short and connected with nothing but the air. The light from the fire momentarily blinded Cleave until the Cyclops drew his huge pumpkin-like face into view and to closer inspect his catch. With his bulbous eye a hands length from Cleave he sniffed and studied the frail Geflack. Struggle as he might, Cleave was a fly in jam now and there was no escape. He tried kicking out again, this time connecting with the Cyclops' bulky chest and proved fruitless in the efforts, the slapping noise from Cleaves lower hands producing only one sure result, making the Cyclops smile.

"Wriggle don't you imp?"

With that he pulled Cleave's arms out till they nearly came off bringing his head in closer. The Cyclops opened his drawbridge like jaw exposing his yellow tombstone sized teeth. Cleave knew his fate was sealed and before his death wished his last moments were not those of this nose being polluted by the smell of rancid Cyclops breath. In a flash the Cyclops bit down and teeth met through a sour pulp. A scarlet gush quenched his thirst then the taste met his tongue, he did not approve. Tossing Cleave's headless corpse at his feet, spitting he cleaned his chin and lips with his forearm wishing to wipe away the bitter taste. Gagging and spitting his words in unison he spoke, "Like rotten fruit, yuck! Have any friends with you?"

The Cyclops scanned the clearing whilst lifting up a branch from the fire to combat the night and causing the shadows to dance away in fear as everything rightly did in his presence. Raith knew he had two options, flee and maybe live, but the opportunity to recruit the Cyclops would be gone, or make himself known before he is detected and appeal to the Cyclops' lust for wealth, provided he had one that is. Raith moved from the shadows with upper hands outstretched to show he had no weapons... Well in his hands anyway.

"I am alone mighty Cyclops and I have a proposition for you."

"Found you little Imp!"

"I found you first and I'm no Imp, I am a Geflack and so was my idiotic friend you just dispatched. Although you did me a favour there so I am in your debt. Allow me to speak freely and tell you my plan so you then may consider the debt paid."

The Cyclops stood towering above Raith, contemplating to squash him or listen. He decided he could listen and then squash him if he liked, so after a sharp snort of acceptance he went back to the area where he had been sleeping, he sat with a ground shaking thud in front of the fire and with his knees up reached across for Cleave's lifeless body. Gripping Cleave's body in his left palm, the Cyclops located a spear that still had some of the merchant stuck to it. He shook the spear away from him removing most of the chunks of merchant and then slowly skewered Cleave's body through his backside till the spear tip emanated from where his head used to be.

"Might taste better cooked."

With that he held Cleave's corpse over the flames and nodded at Raith showing him he was listening and as the

Cyclops picked burnt bits of meat from his spear and chewed disdainfully, Raith explained the plan to capture the Myon, not forgetting to put emphasis on how richly he would be rewarded for his help and explaining how they would need further accomplices. The Cyclops listened and stared in awe at the Geflack as he explained, riches did indeed arouse him and he was definitely keen on this new adventure.

Cyclops: "I'm in, my name Arden, what you called?"

Raith: "Glad you can join my new friend, my name is Raith and I think together we will be rich."

The Cyclops grinned like a simpleton, unaware he was just a pawn in a greater more sinister plan. Raith suggested they stayed where they were tonight and move out before first light in the morning, keeping to the forest and moving to a tavern which lay in the direction of the Myon's last whereabouts. The tavern is only open through the night and known to hold every scoundrel, thief, murderer and bastard of these lands, there they would surely find another bounty hunter to join their crusade.

Chapter 14

The unlikely duo skulked through the undergrowth moving west as Raith had planned, the weather began to get noticeably colder and the glass breaking sounds of ice pools under the Cyclops' gigantic feet did betray their whereabouts, but nothing was in earshot to respond apart from the odd owl. Raith preferred to stay high in the trees, dancing from branch to branch and moving further ahead as a scout, he knew his sizable companion would be spotted sooner than he and to be able to keep out of sight and danger was preferable to trying to make small talk with the beast. For two days they moved this way, Raith on point and Arden bringing up the rear; they rested in caves and under fallen trees when they had to, but they were isolated in these parts and that's how they preferred it. Finally, as dusk fell on the third day, Raith spotted black smoke piercing the clouds, the trees began thinning as were common around any sorts of populations. Wood was felled for building materials and for fuel which would leave areas too open for Arden to cross. He was rightly feared by most races and Raith knew he would have to approach the tavern alone, he could blend in and his size would make him forgettable, little did anyone know what powers he now had, the might of a Cyclops at his disposal.

Arden and Raith backtracked so they could talk unheard by the taverns comers and goers, a light snow had begun to fall and the bushes started looking like they had been finely dusted with flour.

Raith spoke, "If we are to find a third, it will be here my friend, best you stay put and wait for my signal, if I don't come out by morning, let your rage lose like thunder and flatten the tavern."

"Sounds more fun than waiting here, I should do it now!" Arden said with the moon beginning to shine up his massive blood lusting eye.

"We need more for our hunting party, at least let me try to recruit and then you may have your fun if I fail."

"Fine, but if you need me just shout."

Raith didn't like having to explain himself to a Cyclops, but he knew it was better to keep him calm and under thumb, a weapon like this must be handled carefully.

As darkness grew to night, Raith stood in his cloak and hood watching the tavern in the shadows, he was now camouflaged in to the scenery in a white veil of snow. His breath was the only thing that could be seen and even that was evenly dispersed by the overhanging foliage. When the moon was high and music could be heard, he knew now was his time to approach, patrons had stopped entering for a while now and the merriment inside was well underway.

Circling around and approaching from the front like he had just wandered past like anyone else, Raith had to make his steps harder to the ground than normal, being heard coming people inside would be at ease, to just suddenly appear would cause suspicion.

Raith had to reach up to turn the iron latch on the solid wooden door of the tavern and as he pushed it open, the smell of food and the warmth were as deafening as the unknown melodies being drunkenly smashed out on an ancient, dilapidated piano. The innkeeper was rushing to pour ale into jugs and the wenches trying not to spill it when rushing it to the tables and trying to avoid getting their arses slapped by every drunken fool staggering between tables. The innkeeper was a human, Raith despised these creatures more than most, useless and without skill their best use was like this one, ale provider. He looked to Raith and hurriedly pointed to a table and stool low enough for his kind in the corner furthest from the piano. Raith nodded his shrouded face and moved quickly out of the path of an oversized human holding two jugs of ale he had relieved the wenches of and he laughed loudly as they were trying to get them back and kept getting greeted with his pox riddled face all screwed up for a kiss.

Raith sat with his back to the wall observing his surroundings; plenty of little exits as he liked to see should trouble arise he could stab, slash and disappear, the Geflack way. As the evening drew on he barely supped his ale and from a distance was surrounded by a translucent calm that seemed to protect him from the chaos around him. As the hours moved by, the noise reduced, patrons left or stole wenches to the upper chambers and even their revolting noises of love seemed to subside. Raith had been eyeing a cloaked figure all night, he had caught a glimmer of pale greenish-blue skin that was deliberately being hidden and the occasional lock of dark brown hair would be brushed back under its hood.

Now the majority of the creatures and humans frequenting the tavern had either past out from drink or had left, the cloaked figure and Raith seemed now to share the same translucent protective bubble and when the figure glanced in Raith's direction, he did not look away, feeling safer this time that it might be indeed OK to reveal himself and his intentions. For what seemed like an hour, but which was actually seconds they sized each other up, neither removing one's hood and both just seemingly fixated on the darkness in each other's hoods. Suddenly an upper door burst open and out staggered two sizable humans bearded and singing, their demeanours spouted arrogance and as they left their doorway making their way down stairs to the bar, Raith noticed a wench sobbing from inside their room. They meant to carry on their boisterous evening with more ale. Barely making it down the stairs they didn't even notice Raith in the shadowy corner and slammed in to the bar felling several stools as they did so.

The first drunkard belched as he shouted and struck the bar with an open hand whilst his companion stood with a wide gait trying to steady himself under the influence and overweight.

Drunk 1, "Ale!"

Drunk 1, "ALE! Damn your eyes!"

"Coming sir, coming." Was the response from the innkeeper.

The innkeeper quickly served up two jugs of foamy ale and both the drunkards clasped their own with both hands and gulped heartily before belching loudly. One of the men struggled to focus his eyes on the almost empty room, but then he stopped swaying and focused on the cloaked figure Raith had been fixated on.

"CHEERS!" Drunk 1 shouted, lifting his jug to the figure.

He staggered and waited for a response.

"I said cheers you! What's the matter, Dwarf got your balls?"

By this time both the drunks were fixated on the figure; they looked at each other and in a unanimous agreement and made way for the table where the cloaked figure sat. When they reached its table the figure did not move, face still hidden and fixated on Raith.

Drunk 2 spoke up, "Oi, my friend here asked you a question, you got no balls then?"

The figure slid back its hood with a jerk of its head revealing a stunning green skinned elf woman. Her complexion was flawless and petite. Her skin shimmered purples and reds in the candlelight like oil on top of a blacksmith's water trough.

The elf woman replied, "No balls indeed."

Both drunks staggered back in shock then straightened their backs and puffed out their chests in their best attempts to pretend sober and unshocked at the sight of an elf.

Drunk 1, "An elf bitch then is it?"

Drunk 2, "And a pretty one, I bet she loves big men like us."

The drunken duo laughed and congratulated each other with slaps and pats to each other's backs feeling they were both so clever and witty in their remarks.

The elf woman spoke in a soft but directed manner, strong and fearless and never breaking the stare of Raith. He was too shocked as the humans by her race, but unlike them, he would live to bask in her beauty again.

Elf woman, "Get back to mistreating wenches you piles of horse dung, before you get your rags spoilt with your own blood!"

The drunks both stopped laughing instantly and moved to be each at her either side, they each had exposed a dagger strapped to their oversized waists and had moved their hands so they flickered at their sides ready to make a grasp for her arms.

Drunk 1, "Feisty bitch needs breaking in!"

Both the drunken fools made a dash for her, to seize her arms in an attempt to render her helpless. As soon as they moved, she fired herself back off the stool and stood with her back against the wall and side against the open fire, half her body was bathed in shadow and all that Raith could see clearly, was the twinkle of two very thin blade tips at her sides by her knees. As the drunkards slammed in to each other and realized where she was, one forced the other out of his way and ran forward with arms outstretched to make a grab for her. In a flash of sliver and then crimson, she had moved to her attackers left leaving the first standing looking at his fingers lying scattered around his feet. He lifted both hands to his face to realize she had removed all his fingers in one swoop and all that remained were his fat little thumbs and a scarlet gush spraying from where his fingers used to be. He staggered back and turned to show his friend the predicament inhaling deeply for a drunken roar of agony. As he bellowed his companion turned to face the grinning beautiful elf, she stood like a true warrior slightly side facing, showing one side of her hair tightly plaited to the side of her head to keep it from her eyes when loosing arrows. She stood with both blades back at her thighs, a sticky droplet dangled from her right knife like wax dripping from a candle.

The second attacker, overwhelmed with fury, clasped a bar stool and threw it at her face, barely moving at all she judged its mark and effortlessly tilted her head so it went soaring past causing the innkeeper to duck as it broke where he had been standing in panic against the wall behind the comfort of his bar. Frustrated, he drew his dagger and charging forward he held the dagger outstretched in an effort to pierce her belly, but as he closed the gap she landed a front kick to his dagger driving the blade still in his hand up into his own face slicing his lips and one eye and in the same motion moving from his trajectory. He continued past her as he was rushing at full tilt, but he had dropped his dagger and clasped his blood spilling face. As he passed her, she side stepped and sliced deep into the back of his head tickling his brain with her steel. His run slowed and he stood swaying for a moment before crashing dead through a table. She turned to face her first attacker only to witness the door and half the wall coming splintering in like a hail storm.

Shielding her eyes with her forearm and stepping to escape from the blast she moved her arm to expose a Cyclops, panting and raging, drool covering his chin and ravenous desperation emanating from his eye. He spotted the Elf's first attacker who was missing his fingers; he grabbed the drunkard by the scruff of the neck and forced his head into the open log fire holding it there till the gurgled screams stopped. Just as the Elf was scanning the room for an exit she spotted a cloaked Raith in front of the beast, arms outstretched and visibly trying to calm him. The Cyclops dropped the charred pulp of a man and stood facing the Elf warrior; Raith turned to face her and lifted his hood showing his bulbous Geflack head.

"My friend here heard the screams of your attackers and thought I was in danger, he will not harm you. Before more arrive to inspect this commotion I suggest we leave, come with us, I have a proposition for you."

As Raith and Arden left the tavern, shouts and horns were heard bellowing from the distance, trouble was coming! She sheathed her blades and quickly ran to where she had sat, collected a long cloth bag from the wall which housed her bow, arrows and other supplies and slung it over her head and shoulder slipping into it as it came to rest on her back, she pulled up her hood and dashed out into the night in keen pursuit of most unlikely pairing she had ever come across.

Chapter 15

Several hours of silent running followed, through bushes and forest, over paths and trails, ever changing direction and fighting against the blinding blankets of snow that had once again arrived to cover the land in white. Finally after the last shouts of their pursuers died away into the distance, Arden's gigantic strides shortened and his panting became louder as he struggled against the chill to regain his breath. Raith bounced down from the branches and landed slightly in front of Arden to assume his dominant position as he truly saw himself as the leader of the pack now. Arden had burst into the tavern to help as he was instructed; Raith doubtlessly had himself a most dangerous pet and now a warrior as a third, this was enough to track and capture the Myon despite what Kadamlic had instructed, they were well on their way now and Raith smiled to himself at the thought of success, perhaps he would take the elf woman as his personal guard after all this is over that is if she could be brought to heel.

Raith, whilst in mid-stride, pointed to a dense part of the forest which despite the fact the sun was on the up, no light could enter through such brush. This would be a great place to hide and move further undetected to the last known location of the Myon. Plus he still needed to bring the woman up to speed, if she did not join him, well then he would just give her to Arden, he would surely play rough.

Raith and the woman stood awaiting Arden's return, he had hung back to cover their entrance to the forest and make sure there were no followers to their whereabouts. Slowly he strode in and glanced at them both before sitting in a heap at their feet, Arden was exhausted; a creature his size was used to surprise attacks, not bounding through the forest like a deer. He turned his back to them and soon gave off the repetitive breathing of a sleeping bear. Raith sat with his back against Arden as a very useful windbreak and motioned for the warrior woman to join him. Without a sound she seemed to float towards him and sat like a feather coming to rest. Despite her not being a Geflack, he did find her strangely alluring, but he put this from his mind to concentrate at the task at hand.

Raith spoke, "No fires, but Arden makes a good windshield... So what do I call you?"

She lifted her eyebrows to look at him with her arms sat on top of her knees. "My name is Kornelija, the mountain is Arden, what's your name Geflack?"

"Ha! You know my race?! Call me Raith."

"Yes I know of your kind, strange to see you without a clan and in such... company. So you spoke of a proposition?"

"I have a clan; they wait for me to return from my mission. Arden joins to fight with me for the spoils, tell me, are your skills for hire."

"Ha! Little Raith you know very well that tavern was where blades for hire often go and with a Cyclops at your disposal, I'm guessing the reason you need a quiet blade is because your prey isn't the simple, stupid kind."

"Indeed. I seek a Myon, he wounded my king, I am to return him to face his destiny, gold is the reward, will you join me?"

"Did not think Myons' were around anymore? Would be nice to finally see one I suppose. So yes I will join, but I get twice my weight in gold for such a risk as a Myon, I know you Geflacks' pillage more than that in a month."

"Deal. Now get some rest Kornelija, we are not far from where the Myon was last seen and I'm told he's a tough one."

Kornelija tossed her hood over her head and rested her chin on the backs of her arms that made a bridge between her knees. She sat a little way away from the Raith and Arden, not only did she not trust Raith, a Geflack who were known as deal breakers and back stabbers, Arden smelt like a dead goat so to sit in the breeze was defiantly preferable. Raith watched Kornelija as she got comfortable, when her last movements to find comfort died and she rested for sleep, he stared at her deep in thought. If this wench thinks she can have twice her weight in gold, she's simple, but I'll settle for her weight in iron chains.

Chapter 16

They slept through the day and travelled at night, the snow always seeming to attempt to blind their path favouring Ackrehm, but onward they trekked. Arden and Kornelija never quite knew the exact location of the Myon, but following the Geflack's lead; Raith in front skipping from branch to branch, Arden slowly striding along and Kornelija cautiously following from the rear.

At dusk, Kornelija shot a hare, but they had to eat it raw due to not wanting to light fires, this would draw unwanted attention and this was the last thing they needed if they were to surprise the Myon. Finally, at the end of the second night, Raith instructed they should halt and he would go on to examine the road up ahead. This was the very road where Kadamlic and his Geflacks had ambushed the Myon some weeks back and Raith wanted to examine the scene, but not much was visible from the weeks of snow that had followed, the Myon's cart was still in pieces and easily found. Raith checked the area and it looked like no other travellers had passed this way, it was after all a very remote area, they had passed but one old woman on a horse since they left the noises of the tavern's pursuers, Arden wanted to eat her but Raith had instructed him not to at his great distaste. On returning to the warrior and the mountain, Raith beckoned they follow and cautiously they obeyed, moving slowly down the path to the destroyed cart and onward to a clearing leading deep into the ice kissed abyss.

Kornelija began to doubt the story Raith had spun whilst Arden had slept, of the Myon attacking the Geflacks' out of pure spite as Raith would have her believe. Raith claimed the cart belonged to his King Kadamlic, but Geflacks were never known to travel in carts, still she was being paid to do a job so she put these doubts from her mind and followed their little leader off the track and into the wilderness. They continued to move late in to the morning instead of sleeping in the day like before. They were alone out here and it seemed sense to Raith to keep moving until at last grey smoke could be seen rising in the distance; Arden spotted this too and grunted in its direction.

"Camp fire!" Arden said, nodding which way to go.

"The fire is out; grey smoke means the fire is out," Kornelija suggested.

"Out or not it's probably the Myon, follow me," Raith said.

Raith skipped up a tree for a higher look, moving nimbly with his four hands, he paused to scan the area and narrowed his eyes. He still found focusing in the daylight hard for his nocturnal eyes. Bouncing back down he landed at Arden's tree trunk legs and told him to stay put as before, "When I need you, I'll shout," he said. Raith looked to Kornelija and nodded in silent instruction that her presence was required and she was to join him, so together they moved forward through branches and thicket to the Myon's hideout.

They came across a small babbling stream that had been recently attended for fishing due to the makeshift dam and small nets hanging from saplings growing near the stream.

They both skulked in the bushes and saw the grey smoke of the extinguished fire piercing the midday sky. Raith noticed the door of a hide sunk into the rocks, he grinned and felt like a spider with a fly in its web, he felt his prey was trapped and was at ease with his companions to protect his skin. Feeling as big as Arden, he motioned Kornelija to stay put with a downward open palm and moved out in to the open, brushing the snow from his ears and head as he went. Slowing walking toward the door, Raith kept his eyes moving and scanning everywhere as he went, cautious and arrogant he approached the door.

"That's far enough Geflack!" Ackrehm spoke in a strong, confident voice, he had seen the small group approaching from the mountain in which his hut was sunk, he had seen the sun shimmer from the Elf's flesh, had seen the branches moving before betraying the Cyclops and had seen the little shape out in front that was Raith. Ackrehm had seen all of this and not fled, but moved down to his hideout to await his guests.

Raith spoke, "So Myon, you are in after all I see, will you come out and talk with me?"

"You Geflack have nothing I want to hear, so leave now and you will live."

"Come now, as you know we Geflacks do not travel solo, so before I have a hundred of my kind break in your door and drag you out in to the snow, will you not come out on your own accord?"

"Ha! You think me stupid imp! I know you travel with a group, but it is no hundred! An Elf and a Cyclops, but not a hundred."

Raith's eyes widened and he swallowed, the Myon knew his group, despite his caution, the Myon saw them coming.

This was inconvenient, but no matter; a Cyclops is stronger than a thousand Geflacks.

"Clever, clever Myon, but you know I have a Cyclops, a big one too. So before I have him open your door, come out and speak."

"Your master has sent you on a death mission, beat down this door and seal your fate, you and yours. Leave now and say you could not find me, this is your best choice."

Raith sighed with frustration, he had hoped to get this Myon in to the open. A shot from Kornelija and he would be more manageable for transportation, oh well he thought.

Raith shouted, "ARDEN!"

His voice echoed through the hills and the cliffs causing birds in neighbouring trees to flutter off and snow to spray from their perches. A few eerily quiet seconds passed then distant branches could be heard snapping, louder and louder this became and a roar could be heard, Arden was coming. Like an avalanche he came, decimating small trees and bushes underfoot until he came exploding through the trees like a comet. Drooling and roaring like a ravenous bear on its hind legs he stood with his arms outstretched to extend his already mountainous stature. He looked to Raith for instruction for he saw no threat or foe.

"Arden, be so kind and open the door."

Chapter 17

Raith pointed towards the Myon's hideout and Arden grinned with excitement, relishing the kill to come. He stomped over to the door, arms swinging as he went like a battering ram made flesh, he looked down to the door, far too small for him to enter then struck out with the flat of his palm. The door shook and cracked, but did not open. It was blocked from the inside. Ackrehm had expected a visit for some time now and had been preparing. He had found a second entrance to his temporary home and begun moving rocks to this front door, blocking it up tight to allow him ample escape time should he need it. Arden, furious, hit again and as before the door cracked and splintered, but did not open. With a shout of anger Arden kicked the door and hammered his fists on to the surrounding walls of the hideout shaking the very mountain and causing small pebbles to shower his shoulders like a meteor storm peppering the horizon. Harder and harder he pounded, with his eye tight shut to protect it from the dust and debris, shouting and drooling like a caged dog smelling meat. Raith looked on and grinned at his beast making short work of this Myon's cave, suddenly Kornelija came rushing from the bushes, waving her arms is distress.

"Look out! From above you fool!"

Raith looked up and saw a gigantic boulder coming loose and just about to begin its descent rapidly to the head of Arden. Raith began shouting too, but Arden was too rage stricken to hear. Kornelija saw but one way to get his attention and loosed an arrow into his backside. He spun like lightning and fixed his eye on her. He began moving toward her with fists clenched at her injuring him when the boulder missed his head by a breath and crashed to a halt sinking in to the floor from its weight exactly where he had been standing. He staggered back from it with surprise and its shockwave, dumbstruck at nearly being squashed like a bug.

"She tried to warn you Arden, but you couldn't hear her."

Arden reached round and pulled the arrow from his hind quarters tossing it at Kornelija's feet.

"I guess I should thank you?" was Arden's response.

"Just in future try keep some control, you will live longer."

Arden was angry at her words of disrespect to him and the arrow stung, still she had saved his life so he would let it go, for now anyway.

Raith spoke, "He's a clever one this Myon, he must have loosened the rocks above for this very reason, there will be an escape route he's taken; Kornelija please find it so we can continue on our mission."

She nodded, glanced at Arden and gave a dry smile, did a little mocking curtsy and dashed off in to the bush surrounding the mountain looking to circumnavigate it and find the Myon's escape route. She was quietly impressed at his ingenuity, but sped on to her goal.

She appeared higher up the mountain and threw a small stone to Raith's feet to get his attention, he looked up pretending it did not startle him quite as much as it did and observed her gesturing, and they followed the path she took; Raith went first and Arden followed, brushing dust from his chest and arms, then scratching the arrow hole in his arse with his left hand as he walked muttering under his breath. Raith ignored his mood, was better to leave the beast to cool in his own time, he was too simple to listen to reason. Finally, they met Kornelija at a well walked path the Myon had recently used to make good his escape. They could see his footprint in the snow and he looked to be wearing a long cloak judging by the drag marks. They all stood for a moment looking into the direction he had fled, down the mountain side and into the forest he went and in the blink of an eye, Raith set off at pace, followed by Kornelija and a disgruntled Arden. Raith thought as he ran, how he was secretly glad the Myon was clever, more of a challenge worthy of his time.

Chapter 18
The Dwarf

Ackrehm had prepared a small holdall of supplies, he knew it was only a matter of time before he would need to leave and as he pounded the snow with his feet, he thought of Therd, he was still angry at the loss of his friend. Maybe one day he would get a chance to express this anger on the King's head, but for now survival was the only focus. He crossed streams, went around frozen ponds, through the thickest ferns and squeezed through rock falls that had closed the path. The now high moon lit his way, but thunder sounded in the distance and like his pursuers, a storm was coming. He could not hear them, but he knew they were close, every so often a bird would sound startled from a distance behind him, it must be them he thought and on he pressed.

Up ahead, Ackrehm noticed a group of lights flicker, like fire flies only brighter. The closer he got the moon revealed an inn and betrayed a river behind it; turning the sky upside down the moon reflected brightly in the black water and Ackrehm made his way in for a closer look. Perhaps a boat moored would give him a nice head start on his unwelcome companions, a chance to put some good distance and perhaps time to prepare a trap or ambush, to turn the tables in his favour, a chance to be the hunter rather than the hunted.

As he approached the inn, he could smell meat roasting, the smell seemed to stroke his face and welcome him in, and he moved to the doorway and eyed the splits in the wood. Inside, a dwarf sat in front of a bar, puffing white smoke from his red and bulbous nose. He sat there waiting for customers or at least for someone to converse with. Dwarves were a hard race and stubborn, but fair in trade and hospitality, you just had to make sure not to mention height or their manners, easily offended and quick to violence Ackrehm would be sure to be careful.

The Myon pushed open the door with purpose and stepped into the warmth, closing the door tight behind him; the Dwarf nodded to the Myon, still smoking and eyeing up his visitor, then the Dwarf spoke in a rough and brash manner as was customary for his kind, "A Myon it would seem, good eve rare one, a bed or just brandy?"

"Sanctuary, Master Dwarf."

"Ahhh and what makes you think you will find that here?"

"I do not wish to bring trouble to your door, but it does indeed follow me. Loan me a boat to get my distance and properly defend myself, I will pay what I can and if not return with the rest."

"And return you would Myon, but you don't look like you travel with gold and I'm no boat owner, the brewers transport the beer upstream, if they should drop a barrel off to me once in a while, then a few glasses in return is all that's asked. Who follows?"

"A Geflack," (the Dwarf sniffs), "an Elf woman," (the Dwarf spits on the floor in disgust), "and a Cyclops."

"A one eye!? Bastards eat dwarfs! I am Didget and here friend you have found sanctuary."

Didget hopped down from his stool and motioned for Ackrehm to follow with a swipe of his pipe hand. As Ackrehm followed through the eye-stinging smoke he noticed Didget's club leaning against the wall, bless this stranger, surely he cannot possibly be willing to risk his life for someone he does not know? They walked through the storeroom of cured meats and bed linen, through a door and down in to the darkness toward the sound of water. They were on a platform at the back of the inn, a barrel floated in the water, occasionally clonking against the platform as the waves brushed against it.

"They were not far behind," Ackrehm said.

"Hide here, keep quiet and if all turns to mud, slip out in the stream."

"Why help?"

"You're a Myon, maybe the last? And a Cyclops is coming; I've wanted to kill one again for years…"

Ackrehm could tell the dwarf smiled by the rising crease in his beard; Didget turned and scurried up the stairs turning a key in the door behind him. The Dwarf's footsteps sounded muffled from inside, but Ackrehm was comforted by the knowledge his whereabouts was unknown, for now anyway, then came a creaking, slowly and softly as the front door of the inn was being opened.

Chapter 19

Didget had returned to his stool and continued to puff as the door to his inn opened with a care. A moment passed before Raith and Kornelija stepped in from the rain that had begun to pour down like a waterfall since the Myon had arrived.

Raith spoke with a false smile and tone, the pleasantry seeming uncomfortable and bitter to his lips and even more so to the Dwarf's ears.

Raith: "I am looking for a friend of mine."

Didget: "HA! Not found here I'm sure."

Kornelija: "This is the only shelter around from the rain, he's here."

Didget: "Ahhhh, but its only just started raining Elf, so your friend will likely be out there wetter than you."

Raith: "If he's here then tell us so we can all leave together."

Didget: "As I said, not found."

Didget folded his arms in defiance and smirked under his beard knowing that this was the quickest way to get to meet the Cyclops. Raith smiled and slowly moved to the left of the entrance and in the same move, Kornelija moved to the right. A dripping, hairless paw gripped the inside of the door frame and the Cyclops's pumpkin sized head leered in from the darkness. Pulling his body through, Arden broke the door frame but finally stood at full high in the cramped bar, he had smelt the dwarf and was dying to come in for a look. He stood as a leaning tower over the Dwarf, dripping all over from the rain outside and staring deep into the dwarf's expressionless beard.

Raith: "Arden, please ask the Dwarf where our Myon is."

Arden grinned and his pupil shrunk in size as he leaned in with a look of domination towards the dwarf. Arden snatched for the dwarf only to clasp the stool he had been sitting on as Didget had darted out of the way and out of sight laughing as he went.

Didget: "Too slow trout breath!"

Throwing the stool behind him, Arden placed one hand on the bar and tried to feel under it with the other, reaching in every corner and crevice for the dwarf. Didget had collected his club and spotted Arden's clumsy big hand on the bar; like a lightning flash and just as powerful, Didget welted Arden across his knuckles, hearing one pop like a dry old walnut shell. Arden let out a mighty roar, clasping his hand like a bear with a paw full of hornets and stepping back from the bar. Cursing and swiping with his good hand at a glimpse of the dwarf, he again missed and swiped a table against the wall. Didget moved to his blind side and struck the Cyclops across his right knee cap sending the mountain crumbling to the floor, tumbling through tables and sending wooden shards scattering while he was writhing in agony. Lying on his back he opened his eye to see Didget upside down looking back at him with his long beard tickling his nose.

The Dwarf spoke with deep booming disrespect that shadowed his meager size, "Time to piss your cloth at the sight of a Dwarf you waste of skin!"

But before Didget could deal the final blow and crush the Cyclops's head like an egg, a reflection in the Cyclops's eye seen too late paints the dwarfs' fate in the form of Kornelija, the forgotten assailant to this towering oaf wielding a broken table leg with blinding speed towards his averted glaze, then darkness.

Didget sharply came screaming back to reality with a mug of stale mead to the face; coughing and spluttering he struggled to wipe the blurring from his eyes but his hands were bound. He attempted to kick but his legs were bound also. The Dwarf was lying horizontally roped to his own bar, he turned his head to the side and his eyes began to clear. He could see the Geflack sat on his stool grinning away, the Cyclops standing near the door holding his broken fingers and the Elf leaning over him looking down.

Kornelija: "Welcome back."

Kicking and struggling as he spoke, his forehead turned red as a hot poker and steam was expected to emanate from his ears due to rage. "Untie me you bastard cowards and feel a dwarf's rage!"

"Now calm yourself you talking beard, we have some questions for you."

She stood looking down with her dazzling opal eyes, heaving busty depiction of an elfish warrior woman. Glancing over to the Cyclops who was drowning his defeat and numbing his paw with beer she spoke with a scary hypnotic trance that seemed to penetrate deeply into Didget's mind.

"That was quite a feat felling our mighty oak."

The Dwarf looked to the Cyclops then back to the Elf giving her his cheeky, sparsely toothed grin. "There's more where that came from, care to see, whore?"

"Now, now, let's not make me have to slice the tongue from your hairy little cantaloupe; at least not before you've had a chance to spin me a yarn, I know how your kind loves a story."

"The only thing you'll get from me is a cracked head pretty one."

Stepping back and never breaking eye contact, Kornelija squatted and swiftly scooped up a thick, sharp wooden splinter and began spinning it comfortably between her delicate, but skilful fingers. With certain smoothness like walking on a beach she approached Didget, placing one hand on his forehead and hovered the spike over his right eye, then to his left. Backwards and forward from eye to eye she moved the spike, humming a childlike tune as she went.

"Now then, tell me the tale of the Myon we seek and you shan't end up like my friend over there," motioning with her head in the Cyclops's direction.

"I don't need eyes to break that pretty face of yours, a Dwarf's club always finds its mark."

Kornelija released his forehead and exhaled with frustration. Didget found her warm sweet breath intoxicating, a drug he thought as he shook it from his head.

"Brave, stubborn and dim as are all stone miners."

"Stone-Miner?! Do you see a pick in my hands?"

"No master Dwarf I do not."

Quicker than he could blink, she pinned his left forearm to the bar with her empty hand and nailed his palm to the counter top with a single, lightning powerful stab of the wooden spike. Didget erupted like a volcano with roars, abuse and saliva.

"Ahhhhhh! You bitch, you will pay for this!"

Raging with pain, globules of spit clung to his beard like rain drops on a cobweb. His nose ran as he panted to subside the pain and gritting his jaw to regain his composure.

"Now I ask again, the Myon, where might he be hiding?"

Didget fixed her sedated gaze, jaw bulging from his biting down so hard, he noticed she had another spike already in her hand and she mockingly scratched her head with it in pretend boredom and dramatically yawned to add emphasis to the fact she was losing interest and was not at the least bit interested in how much pain he was in. She walked around the bar, both parties fixed on each other's eyes, hers hypnotically calm and his burning with rage like the forge fire within his soul. Again without him having time to flinch she held his right forearm to the bar and smiled holding the stake aloft.

Kornelija: "Well?"

Didget remains silent in defiance and she stabbed down again pinning his remaining palm to the bar. Try as he might to ignore the pain it became too much, the pain grew filling his body with an acrid acid that flowed from his mouth in another mighty roar.

Didget: "Ahhh Damn you all!"

Biting his bottom lip for relief he sobered from the pain momentarily, moving eyes from the Elf to the Geflack and the Cyclops as they approached his body. The Geflack hopped on to a stool and they all looked down at him, eyes filled with the blood lust of a pack of wolves. Moving his eyes he studied their features and then in a strong but croaky refusing voice he spoke. "I am not afraid to die, I know you will kill me even if I do tell you what you want, so best I don't. Kill me well for my spirit will return and peel the wretched skin from your already dead forms."

He signed off his speech by spitting at the Elf praying to hit her beauty and somehow forever leave his mark and a taint on her lustre, but due to her cat-like speed he missed, to his eternal dismay.

"Enough talk!" Raith hopped up on to the bar and grasped a clay bottle, removing the cork with a pop and pouring the very strong smelling brandy over Didget's restrained body; Kornelija lost Didget's gaze and stood fixated on Raith.

Kornelija: "This is not how I work."

The Geflack span to face the elf, staring daggers that struck out at her clawing and snagging her like his barbed words.

Raith: "Then leave and forget your coin!"

Motionless, Didget lied in acceptance of his incumbent fate until Raith lifts the oil lamp from the ceiling hook above them and smashed the glass container down at Didget's feet.

Hiding down in the cellar Ackrehm heard the screams, stifled and muffled by the flames until they ceased and a faint, high pitched squeal was the only sound that filled the air of the soul leaving the defiant and loyal Didget. Ackrehm asked himself why on earth the dwarf protected him as the smell of burning meat and hair leaked down to his position and his nostrils bringing him away from such thoughts. Ackrehm lowered himself in to the river and slipped away in to the cold bitter wake of the river's current, silently sweeping his broad arms through the liquid darkness allowing its strength to carry him away from this madness.

Raith stood watching the tavern burn, the flames reflecting a perfect image of the horror in his midnight eyes and burning deep inside him, the taste of destruction and leadership had lured him to wicked extremes and he liked it.

Kornelija waited out of sight watching the fires and Raith, she was momentarily troubled by what had happened, but she put it from her mind and tried to focus on keeping a close watch on Raith, he would set his beast Arden on her should he so wish and her speed would count for nothing if she did not see it coming; she watched the Cyclops come running from the shadows and reporting to Raith,, what an obedient pet he was turning out to be.

Arden: "Can't find, only fire... and a river."

Raith: "Then that's where he went slipped away like an eel, we follow the river; tell the Elf and from now on she needs to be watched."

Arden grunted with acknowledgement and beckoned Kornelija, she had already overheard the plan and of course about how she will be watched, well that's fine she thought, she would be watching them both right back. Marching off like the conqueror of an empire, Raith walked taller than before and he felt like a king, Arden quickened his pace overtaking Raith to clear the route of any surprises. Kornelija almost floated along behind the pair, silently placing one foot in front of the other and moving in her Elf-like manner, her eyes piercing in to the back of Raith's head. Her daring to try read his mind and anticipate his next moves, walk tall now little lord she thought, she had had dealings with over confident sadists before and she would not be bested by this one.

Chapter 20
The Banshee

The currents had taken Ackrehm quiet far, but the cold was killing him and he needed to get out of the icy water. He kicked his legs allowing him to reach a near bank and he hauled himself through muddy silt till he was aloft from the icy embrace off the river. He rolled over a few times in the snow to take most of the water off him, an old trick his father taught him just in case he ever fell in the water when ice fishing. Still trembling and watching his breath rise in the moonlight, he trekked off through the knee deep snow, exhausting himself with every laboured step, he knew he must keep moving for his pursuers would be not far behind and he needed to gain distance on them.

Ackrehm stooped ever forward into the darkness, the ice wind cutting his brow like a frozen whip and the dark of the night swallowed his entire being, it pressed against his eyelids and flooded his nose, it filled his soul like being poisoned, stiffening his limbs with fatigue. He thought he could make out flickers of fire torches in the distance behind him, but they had disappeared as quickly as he had noticed them. Was it the band of hunters hot in his pursuit or the results of a sub-zero mind playing elusions? He needed to find shelter and sanctuary, but he could see neither in the blinding night ahead.

As the compacted snow grew firmer he moved more briskly, taking care not to tread too heavily and aid his already persistent pursuers. After what seemed like ten thousand paces, he came to a mound set in to a small hill. A sheeted door danced frantically in the wind and two dwarf sized cages hung either side, rusty and squeaking they groaned in the wind. Bones littered the entrance of this hovel poking through the snow, but they were too thin and meagre to have belonged to Dwarfs', surely not children? Frozen in horror, Ackrehm stood dumbstruck, he had heard of Banshees who lived out in the vast plains, burrowed into the hills and at night they wandered in search of children of all races to capture, torture and devour. Ackrehm knew that this was not a welcome refuge from the bounty hunters and saw to pass this evil place. Suddenly a low child's voice came from inside the den, calm and sweet it spoke, "I'm lonely, don't be afraid." Ackrehm backed away, he knew by the cold wind and the calm nature that this voice spoke in, this was no child, any young would be scared senseless in such a place.

"Come in," came a voice much deeper and more sinister this time and Ackrehm was terrified, he only came to his senses when from a way off behind came a noise of a beast breathing deeply and moving at pace, the Cyclops! He quickly regained himself and moved silently away and over the hill, a grin briefly emerging on his face as he moved off in to the darkness at the beastly presence that lay in wait for his attackers, perhaps they would not be so lucky as he.

Raith and Arden were walking in unison, Raith using the Cyclops as a gigantic windbreak and Arden using his mighty hand to shield his bulbous eye from the stinging sleet and hail.

Raith spoke as loud as he could, his voice being swept away by the wind like the Myon downstream. "This way, his marks say he came through here."

Slowly Kornelija moved in behind Raith and Arden with her cloak held tight to her body, struggling to keep hold in the violent wind. They pressed on forward and came face to face with the same hill doorway that Ackrehm had avoided only moments earlier.

Arden: "Think he inside?"

Kornelija: "This is a bad place, the Myon wouldn't, would he?"

Raith: "Well if he hasn't, we must, we will freeze out here."

Arden was the first to move forward from the darkness, becoming a shelter and door for the others. He swept aside the mighty cow skin door and allowed the two to go first. Raith held back; he was not stupid, if there were danger inside best let the Elf find it first. She still had her left arm across her body holding her cloak tight, but her right hand was tickling the hilt of her blade, ready to draw it in a flash of lighting and strike just as furiously. "Be ready," she whispered as she went in, a single flame lantern flickered at the back of the wide open room, dancing in the wind from the open doorway, she scanned the room this time with her blade slightly drawn in its scabbard, if she needed to pull it free, it would not make a sound. Raith moved in behind her, poised for the sign of danger to dive for cover and make room for Arden. Kornelija moved further in, silence piercing her ears like her dagger through flesh; Raith had moved to one side and Arden was, as quietly as he could, crawling through the doorway. Finally, when he was inside he could only kneel due to his size, this somewhat restricted his fighting ability, but still he was a force to overwhelm most fully abled opponents. They waited in silence for what seemed like an eternity for either the sign to charge at an enemy or the sight of a fleeing Myon to capture, but neither came and they began to search the den. Raith moved to the lantern at the back of the room producing a small, surprisingly dry, torch from his cloak and holding it to the flames letting it engulf and light his path. It had been impossible to use in the weather outside, but here was perfect. He held it aloft creating sinister shadows that danced around the room as he moved.

"Looks like an old witches' coven," he said as he moved, finding several other wall mounted torches in the room he began the process of lighting them all and bringing light where there was only darkness. The room was simple, an old cot against the wall, some plates and a fire pit in the middle and a strange structure they had passed on their way in. It was covered over with a large sheet made of all off cuts of hides. It had many holes littering its surface and as he moved in for a closer inspection, he could see the rust from bars underneath. It was a cage of some sorts, why he thought would it be covered? Then a movement from inside caused him to jump back. Arden and Kornelija reacted to his fright and were by his side in a flash. Kornelija took the torch from his shaking hand and pushed him back behind her with her free hand. She looked over to Arden who had shuffled forward on his knees to get in to position. Holding the flames closer to the sheet, she drew her blade, looked to Arden and nodded. She stood ready to pounce like a cat as he tore away the sheet throwing dust in the air and their eyes. As the particles fell like snow and shone like stars in the torch light, they all stared at the cage's contents in shock and surprise. Two Dwarfs, uncharacteristically slim and frail looking, they had obviously been here for some time and were suffering from hunger and dehydration. One looked stronger than the other by the way he had his companion's head on his lap, seemingly looking after him and as he spoke in a dry raspy voice, eyes blinking and struggling with the light.

Dwarf 1: "Water, my brother and I need water."

Kornelija moved forward and passed the neck of her drinking flask through the cage, the Dwarf offered up his hand and she poured a pool into it. Even being as thirsty as he was, he first offered the liquid to his brother and weakly he slurped, only then did he put his hand back to the flask allowing her to fill it once more and then drinking himself.

Kornelija: "What is this place, how are you here in this cage?"

Dwarf 1: "Not sure, I am Toad and this is my brother Emall, we were out drinking in a fellow Dwarf's tavern many nights past, we staggered out drunk and collapsed outside and then we awoke here. Sometimes we could hear strange noises, children crying and laughing, all sounding so wrong and evil, I had to fight not to cry out. Emall here has no tongue, even if he were strong enough he could not make a sound."

Raith: "And you've no clue what brought you here?"

Toad: "No, but whatever it is, it's dangerous, to drag two Dwarfs' to such a place, it must be magic."

Raith: "Probably a witch, but gone now we are here. Are you to be trusted if we let you out?"

Toad: "Help us and we will stand with you until the debt is paid."

Raith: "Sounds good to me, Kornelija if you would be so kind…"

Raith could not believe his luck, two Dwarfs to join the hunt, and for free no less. Dwarfs are hardy and when they are strong could be a viable asset, plus when the debt is paid and their usefulness expired, well they could meet the same fate as Kornelija he thought; disposable labour was his favourite kind.

Chapter 21

As Ackrehm was making a slow, but definite distance by braving the cold, his would be captors had set in for the night, torches and fire pit lit, the band littered the edges of the hovel. The Cyclops lay facing the wall, snoring his head off and showing the group his bare backside as he slept. Raith had squatted close by to him, back against the wall and head bobbing, dozing in and out of sleep. Kornelija also sat with her back to the wall, holding her knees and with her chin resting on her forearms. Watching the Dwarfs sleep together closest to the doorway she in particular had been disturbed by their lodgings. Children's bones had scattered most of the floors which she had thrown from the door, but worse was the paintings on the walls, she tried to ignore them, but found her heavy eyes wandering. Flayed skin had been used as canvass to inscribe wicked depictions of a tall shadowy figure holding hands with all different young races. Blood had been used for paint and even though it was now brown and flaking off, nothing could stop her mind drifting to the poor young who had been the inspiration to such debauchery or to the monster that was its creator. Her eyelids faltered and closed, dozing due to fatigue and the rhythmic, almost hypnotic, rasps and snores of her companions.

The Dwarfs slept side by side cocooned in the sheets that once hid them and their cage from view, they huddled together like twins in a womb. They were set up to sleep closest to the door due to the fact neither of the other bounty hunters knew or trusted them, it was Raith's idea to have them nearest to danger should it arrive and furthest away from the rest of the group. Tightly they clutched at the sheet as they slept; blissfully unaware that something had snuck in and joined them. Toad awoke, the lights burned low and visibility was as slim as his brother now was, but he could hear something, a slurping and sucking noise. He blinked several times and listened, holding his breath to hear the noise more clearly; insatiable it persisted, wet and drooling it sounded like a hound at its bowl. Suddenly he noticed a movement at their feet, he sat upright and reached for a torch that hung as low as it burned beside them and brought it into view to illuminate a hunched twitching shape at his brothers' feet. Covered in a grey shawl, it was definitely the source of the sounds. He quickly realized this 'thing' could be harming his brother and he hastily threw back the sheet pushing the flames towards the shape. Frozen with fear he saw nightmares come to life, a Banshee sharply looking back at him, black eyes with an emaciated staring face covered in blood and slurping chunks of pureed flesh. The Banshee had been feasting on his brother's feet and in its claws it held the fleshy skeletonised remains of his brother's extremities. He drew breath to shout for aid when the Banshee let out the most petrifying and piercing scream he had ever heard. As she did so, blood spattered all over his face, momentarily blinding him from the horror; The others were awake in a flash, but so disorientated they had no idea where lay the attack, Toad scurried backwards pushing with his palms to get away from the monster and in a vain attempt to find a weapon with which to defend himself, but when he backed into the wall suddenly and opened his eyes it was gone, away in to the night like a bad dream leaving commotion and horror in its wake.

Arden in the panic and surprise, had tried to jump to his feet, smashing his head in to the low ceiling and now sat in a heap against the wall like an oversize crumpled bear in the summer heat.

Raith: "What's going on, what is it?"

Arden now awake and on his knees was hunched over, holding his bruised head and growling wildly, not only to sound his ferocity to his enemies and to dominate, but because his head span with concussion after knocking himself senseless.

Kornelija: "Toad! What's going on?"

In the dim light armed with a long, thin blade Kornelija had made her way over to the Dwarves, Toad was cradling his brother and rocking slowly.

Toad: "He's dead, bled like a pig by the beast that lived here! My brother, my little brother…"

Raith was over by Kornelija's side to inspect the carnage and whispered in her ear, "How did he not wake?"

"I've heard a Banshee would drug their victims with a sharp talon, and then when it takes effect you're helpless. He was probably awake when it was eating him and could do nothing, looks like he's bled to death."

Kornelija approached the distraughtt Toad and softly spoke in her Elf manner to calm him and control him, "Move your brother back from the door and help me build a fire close to the entrance, it won't come back with fire."

As the fire crackled loudly and the flames licked high to the ceiling, they could hear a distant cry that made them all shiver like having iced water dripping down their spines. The Banshee was screaming and cackling loudly in the distance, it echoed all around and sounded like it came from all over as it bounced over the open plains, cold and shrill the screams infected all who heard it with despair and abandonment. Toad had covered his brother with the sheet from their cage and sat staring at the fire, hate and anger building inside; he had recovered his brother's small but broad single headed axe from their belongings that the banshee had tossed aside on their arrival and as he sat holding this weapon, the light danced with his anger, bouncing off the blade and his glassy eyes fighting with each other as the dwarf fought with his inner rage and his last remaining hold on reality. Raith watched him intently and like a vampire wanted to drink in his pain; now this little Dwarf would have much fight in him he thought, now he was ready to join them for the hunt of the Myon.

Chapter 22

The sun had begun to rise, spilling light over the snow covered plains and illuminating the land, warming Ackrehm's frost bitten face. It beckoned him to move forward and encouraged his spirits, giving him hope and a sense there could be light at the end of even the most disturbing night. He had marched all night and put considerable distance between him and his would be captors. He still grinned when he thought of how they must have had so much fun dealing with the Banshee. After all they had not gained on him so they must have taken shelter, a foolish move that worked to his advantage. As Ackrehm moved on towards the red sun peering over the hills he noticed he was approaching a vast cliff face so wide he could not possibly go down, he approached the edge and looked down, he could not see the bottom for the mist, but he knew this was not the path, he would have to move on following the edge to find a bridge or a suitable place to climb down, but with no rope he preferred the bridge idea. Suddenly a bull horn bugle sound pierced the silence and sent birds racing from the mists shooting high into the sky and taking Ackrehm by surprise with them as he jumped out of his skin and nearly straight over the edge. He heard another loud bugle blast and shouting, footsteps rushing in his direction, but there was nowhere to run or hide, he ran one way but heard them coming from this direction, he changed course and still they came, he was surrounded. Ackrehm stood with his back to the vast cliff's edge and readied himself, he knew a fight was coming and this could be his end. He puffed his chest out and the adrenalin burned through his veins like molten steel in a forge, he began to breath deeper, almost panting like an enraged bull being circled by its demise. Humans! They had infected this land only recently, growing in numbers like woodland rabbits and raping the land of all they could take. Like an infection they had spread through the hills, over mountains and across seas. Ackrehm could not stand their kind, all they did was take and it is thanks to races like Humans, that his was nearly extinct. Humans would hunt different species to the point of extinction, or worse still, force them in to slavery. They were not a particularly hardy race, but their numbers swarmed like wasps and grew as endlessly as the ocean's vastness.

Four Men appeared and then five, six, more and more till over twenty could be seen. They had basic amour, some chain mail shirts and gauntlets. Some had helmets and boots, others were barefoot, and all looked exactly what they were, scavengers and traders in flesh. Suddenly a crossbow bolt struck Ackrehm in the right collar, compounding through his flesh and exposing its jagged tip from his back. Ackrehm had to bite down hard but did not scream, the pain fuelled his anger and he became numb to it, a human bellowed from amongst the rabble and they parted down the middle exposing a fat bearded human in finer mail than the others. He stomped forward brandishing a large machete, in a frenzied flail shouting obscenities, as he spat he butchered the maverick archer who saw fit to seize the kill for himself. As the disembowelled grunt slumped over in a moist mess to the floor the Humans' leader turned to Ackrehm smiling at first, but then suddenly panicked when he noticed Ackrehm beginning to sway from the blood loss sustained from his injuries.

Human Leader: "Quick! Get him back from the edge damn your eyes, before he falls!"

The band rushed forward with arms outstretched as if to cover the distance by sheer reach alone, but it was fruitless as Ackrehm's eyes fluttered and he disappeared from sight over the cliff edge.

Human Leader: "Fuck, Fuck, Fuck, you stupid filthy... Ahhhhhhhhhh!"

Beside himself with rage and swiping his machete near anything that moved, the leader was beyond ravenous with anger at the loss of his captured Myon, as the band dispersed in a circle leaving their leader in the centre and taking turns in dodging the swipes from his blades, desperately trying to keep out of harm's way one man had ventured closer to the edge where Ackrehm had fallen and went in for a closer look. He moved his toes closer and closer to the edge then leaned forward investigating over his nose to see if he could look down at the Myon's broken body. Peeking ever so slightly further and at his very full stretch he spotted something low down and close to his own foot, as he drew breath to shout for attention a blooded hand grasped him by the calf and in a flash of an ember he was torn from the ledge. With a deafening high pitched woman-like scream as he plummeted until the unfortunate's head struck off a rock sending a spray of mulch in to the air silencing his wailing forever, the others span to look in his direction and the leader ceased in his ranting. Quickly they all moved to the edge needing orders from their leader to find the courage to glance over the edge, slowly three faces appeared over the edge looking down at the Myon as he clung to the vertical face, battered by the wind as he struggled to open his eyes he looked up and their eyes met.

Human leader: "Get him up here and if he falls, you best jump after him before I get you!"

One stocky human pushed his way to the edge whilst rummaging in a bag he was clutching, "Time to go fishing," he chuckled and after a few moments scrabbling he produced several black barbed hooks used to hang meat to tenderize and dry, also used to ascend hard to reach places, but soon to be used as the most painful helping hands Ackrehm could possibly dream of.

The first hook crashed above the Myon's head, blinding him with showers of stone and dust. As he shook his head to clear his eyes, the debris scratched and burnt like a branding iron. Blindly hanging, he heard several more clinks and scrapes as hook after hook was cast downward until like a fish harpoon one found its mark and that mark being him. A hook crashed in to his back forcing the wind from his lungs and wrenched hard to burrow deep like a forest tick and secure its hold. Then another to the leg and another to the shoulder striking the crossbow bolt that still protruded from his back and sending a shock wave of fire down his body. Fatigued by the pain his grip on the rocks loosened, he slipped away from the edge and dropped only to be immediately suspended like the most twisted and macabre child's puppet in the world. Sharply he began to rise, blacking out momentarily, then awakening again as his ascent scraped his face and broken horn against the rocks, slowly rising a hand at a time until he reached the top. Held by hooks and gripped by fear he looked up at his puppet masters to see the leader's face staring back at him with a gaping grin and rotten teeth.

Human Leader: "Hello my friend, glad we didn't lose you."

With that he struck Ackrehm on the crown with the flat of his machete and sent his face crashing into the stones and his mind spinning into a dream and away from all this pain... for now.

Chapter 23
A Trade

Raith, Arden, Kornelija and Toad left the Banshee's lair in their wake, smoke rising from the distant hovel where they had burnt Emall's body and the horrible den that had seen his demise. As they pressed on, Toad stared onward in deep drunken thought. Even his footsteps were heavy with the weight of his brother on his mind, part of him had died with his brother and what was left was a shell of anger wanting to strike out at anything and everyone. Raith occasionally looking back and grinned, he loved the sense of pain that Toad carried and he knew he could use it, use it like he was using them all to fulfil his selfish need for lustrous power, they needed to find the Myon and take him once and for all. With no brush or trees to hide in they all marched in the open, it was only when the sun was setting that Arden rushed back from his usual position ahead of the group relaying what information he had discovered.

Arden: "There was a fight I think, many footprints and a dead human, but no Myon. They take him?"

Raith: "Humans, all we need."

Kornelija: "Bet they couldn't believe their luck finding a Myon."

Raith: "If he's not dead already they will have him to sell or as a pet. Either way, we need him."

Arden: "Think them nearby, music and shouting from a camp, many Humans."

Raith: "Well then we go to take him back, Kornelija and Toad wait here, last thing we need is for them to get excited at an Elf and Dwarf. Let's see if we can strike a deal. Arden with me!"

Raith and Arden moved off into the sunset leaving Kornelija and Toad to be a sure back up if they were needed; Kornelija was pleased to be away from Raith, his evil soul was growing and she could feel his gaze every time she turned away, but being left with Toad was no better option, he did not speak and an angry Dwarf was quite a dangerous companion, she spoke to him to try and calm his mind but to no avail.

Kornelija: "This will not end well, I know why I stay I am an outcast, but you Toad you should be with your people."

He made no reply, just stared at the dim lit shapes of Raith and Arden fading in to the distance and drank in the anger brewing in his mind from the loss of his brother, she was right he thought, this will not end well, but what did it matter now without his brother.

Ackrehm began to regain consciousness; his head ached like too many nights on wine and he felt sick and dizzy. His eyes were heavy and stung with blood that glued his lids together. He could hear running water and moved his head close to its direction, realizing his hands and feet were bound he crawled and squelched through mud on his belly until the running water was over his eyes, blinking frantically it hurt to open his eyes but his vision was coming back to him. Rolling over on to his back he looked up and saw the source of water was a human standing over his cage and pissing in. Spitting and coughing Ackrehm could hear the bastard laughing as he moved on; rage deafened him causing his pulse to race, but he cleared his head and tried to calm his mind, this was indeed a troublesome situation and rage would only be an enemy, he needed to think how he would get out. He would have to be patient and wait for the right moment, he despised Humans like most other races, they were responsible for vast creature decline and he knew as a Myon, he was a prized possession.

Raith told Arden to hold position as usual in the distance, out of sight as one's strongest card should always be, plus if the guards saw him they would panic and spread like the pox in a brothel and the element of surprise would be lost. Raith waited for dusk to approach and with it came the rain, pounding down like hammers on anvils it cause the floor to dance and spray mud skyward. As Raith's lower hands squelched in the mud, the flickers of their torches became clearer and brighter even with the rain desperately trying to extinguish them.

Two human guards stood watch at a narrow pass of high walls leading in to the human camp, one human was fatter and clearly in charge of his hunched, scrawny accomplice as they enjoyed a pipe under the shelter of the door they guarded. The larger of the two entertained himself by blowing smoke in the hunchback's face stinging his eyes and throat making him cough and get a face full of rain. The fatter human noticed over the coughing and amongst the splashing and dripping, a squelching dominated over the pounding rain. Holding torches in front to light the path, they slowly began to make out a short hooded silhouette.

Fat guard: "Halt! State your business!"

Raith: "Trade."

Hunchback guard: "What have you to trade IMP?"

In a flash Raith threw back his hood baring his death filled eyes and displaying his teeth.

Raith: "IMP I am not! Geflack if you please."

The hunchback gasped and hid behind the barrel of fat that was his senior, clasping his arm and peering around him almost burning him with the torch. The fat man shook his arm free and scowled at the hunchback, hissing something insulting under his breath that was far too distant for Raith to hear. Both the guards stared for a few moments in silence, they were not terrified at the sight of one solitary Geflack, but they were widely known to travel in swarms and their camp could fall to numbers rather than brute force. The fat guard finally realized they had been silent too long and spoke to Raith whilst half facing the hunchback.

Fat guard: "One moment Geflack. Quick go inform..."

The hunchback had already turned and quickly headed off, barging through the door skidding in the mud as he went with one leg seemingly lame forever attempting to keep up with the rest of him. Raith saw this and pondered why they would have such a creature standing guard, hardly a deterrent. Why he was alive baffled the Geflack, for they would drown the crippled and the lame so as not to have drains on their society. Raith was amused how the humans seemed to allow these degenerates to live freely among them; did they pity weakness and infirmity? This would be their undoing.

Chapter 24

Ackrehm was huddled in the corner of his stone cell, water bled through the walls and began to pool at his feet and he did quench his thirst and of course wash the urine from his face. Although cold and refreshing, it hurt his cracked, split lips and his chipped teeth bore nerve endings that were flickering and seeming to bounce pain off his cheeks like lightning bouncing around inside a cloud. He felt around in the darkness for anything to use as a weapon, but nothing came to fruition. He even tried pushing and kicking as quietly as possible against the barred door, but it was solid as an oak and did not budge, gradually he realized he was indeed trapped, he would have to wait for them to expose a weakness then and only then could he make good an escape.

Back at the front gate, Raith simply stood in the rain starring deep in to the fat guard's mind occasionally grinning to try taunt and irritate him. The fat guard was too stupid to notice and continued to look back at the Geflack like he had not a care in the world, however this jovial persona was betrayed by the whistling sound coming from his pipe that had long since been extinguished by the rain and he was too busy pretending not to be bothered by Raith's presence that he had forgotten to light it. Coming crashing through the door slipping flat on his face was the hunchback, he spat out a mouthful of mud and pointed from the floor in Raith's direction. "See my lord, I spoke true, not drunk as you say…"

The human leader marched forward in to the torch light and two other guards in meagre mix match armour holding hammers filled out to stand by his side, but at all times behind him to show respect. As the leader passed the hunchback he accidentally on purpose let a foot swipe his supporting arm sending him back down for another face full of mud and grinning as he did so. Raith liked this, very Geflack like; perhaps this human had potential. The human leader stood attempting to puff out his chest and then quickly glancing back at the hunchback in some sort of an attempt to air his dominance and authority. This Raith was not impressed with, something that has to try so hard is obviously false, but he will play at respect for now, the Myon was the only reason for this interaction.

Human leader: "Good eve there Master Geflack, I am Phobos… Who might you be and how can I help you and your kin?"

"Greetings Phobos, I am Raith and I seek a trade."

"Surely on such a night trade is better sought in a keep?"

"I seek to trade in flesh! My master is in need of a new chariot, what have you that is big and strong?"

Phobos turned to half face his men and spoke loudly to mock Raith and impress his men, to mock a Geflack was considered brave or stupid. "Ha! Tell your master to try an Ox."

Raith stepped closer, cocking his head slightly and pretended to examine the human leader in more detail moving his big eyes over his entire form.

Raith: "You seem under the impression that I am not a serious trade's man or at least that I am alone, which is it human?"

Phobos gulped and turned back to face Raith in full, jest was one thing, but he surely could not risk angering the Geflack as they were not prepared for war.

Phobos: "No, no my friend, you misunderstand me, I take it you mean to procure only the finest transport for your master, it does seem that you have come at an opportune moment for I have acquired one of the finest examples of two legged transport, one I am sure your master and indeed your entire tribe will be impressed by. However, I must warn you, it is wild and will not be cheap."

Raith: "Reliably expensive is it? This would be my masters' favourite kind."

Phobos: "EXCELLENT! Come now sir, come dry yourself by my fire and indeed your master may join."

Raith: "My master currently commands over our clan which need keeping in check and due to our numbers he is regretfully detained. I assure you I speak for all my people and am in high authority to discuss business on my masters' behalf."

Phobos: "Oh I see... But of course come in my friend come warm yourself and eat whilst we talk transport."

Allowing Raith to pass him, the Human leader and his two guards followed through the doorway leaving the fat guard and the hunchback to continue their duties in the pouring rain, they were all too aware they must stand guard should they need to raise the alarm of a Geflack swarm approaching.

Chapter 25

Phobos had lead Raith in to his personal chamber for a discussion away from the others, Phobos could not risk looking foolish again in front of his men; leaderships rose and fell like the sun in human tribes and the unwavering mirage of power must be upheld at all costs. Phobos had positioned two seats close to his open fire, his chair of course being much larger in another feeble attempt at demonstrating seniority. As Phobos sat with a sigh of make believe exhaustion, Raith stood close to the flames with his back turned staring deep in to the dancing flames, focusing on the splintering logs and the occasional shooting embers. He said nothing, his whole pretence was a well thought out plan, not facing Phobos and not speaking would make the human have to approach him carefully, Raith had become the very definition of manipulation and ascendance. He planned to have the upper hand here and would not be out-done by a human, especially one so easily coerced. As he predicted, Phobos could not take the silence and began to broach the void like a small clumsy child attempting to converse with an angry parent.

Phobos: "So… Have you and yours come far?"

Raith left a large pause before he answered; he enjoyed the human's awkwardness and although not facing him, could smell his sweat even in such icy temperatures.

Raith: "It has been a journey, but one well-travelled."

Phobos: "Ha! Excellent to hear my new friend... So you seek transport for your King? Well I have such a rare and wonderful specimen, your King will reward you greatly for finding me."

Raith: "You set high standards human; I do so hope you can live up to them?"

Phobos: "Indeed friend, indeed I can, but of course, there is the matter of... Well as your aware such gems are not cheap so to speak and I must think of my costs to have kept such a rarity as I'm sure you can understand."

Raith turned to face the human leader; the flames shone brightly behind him and swarmed his face in darkness giving just the right sinister presence he was aiming for.

Raith: "For all this boasting of such a prize, you're yet to tell me what you have, I begin to think all this talk must be wind."

Phobos: "Ha! Friend, I have in my possession... A Myon! Would this not make a grand steed for your King? Would you not be respected and praised for such a find? I mean more so than now, a Myon my friend, think of it... Most fear they were all gone, but my stock is the finest."

Raith: "Well a Myon if you do indeed have one, I might be interested in."

Phobos: "Of course you are my good Geflack, but he's not available at present, but he will be very soon."

Raith: "Ahhh so you are all talk, you either have one for sale or you don't, so which is it?"

Phobos: "My friend, I am a businessman, he will be available for sale in two nights, for tomorrow he will fight in our arena, he will cause many to bet wildly and I will not turn down such an opportunity.

Raith: "So you expect me to have him when he's half dead? Insult!"

Phobos: "No, no, no, my friend you misunderstand me, a Myon is strong, even after a fight he will be such a prize, plus the fight will tire him to make him more… Manageable shall we say, at the moment he has such spirit."

Raith: "Very well, I may purchase this Myon of yours on the condition I can watch him fight? And of course his condition will affect the price will it not?"

Phobos: "Certainly you may watch friend and do not fear his condition will be seasoned, but subdued, not broken."

Raith: "So we shall see."

With that, Raith turned back to the flames and Phobos quietly rose from his chair careful not to make too much noise even in his own chambers. He walked to the door deciding it best to offer Raith his quarters for the night, he could go celebrate with some whores and the Geflack would feel rested and generous when it came to bartering for the Myon, at least this was his hope.

Chapter 26
The Pit

Morning came and Phobos slowly opened the door to his chambers peering round the door before he entered to ensure his presence was well received. Raith was sat in the human's chair facing the door and staring at Phobos like he had heard him coming from far away and was waiting patiently.

Phobos: "Do I disturb you friend, did you eat?"

Raith: "I am not disturbed, one of your people left some bread and meat at your door, I trust they were for me?"

Phobos: "Of course my friend, I hope you are rested and well, are you ready to watch the fights?"

Raith: "I am ready to leave, the fight is a formality I must endure to receive the Myon, let us get this over with."

Phobos smiled gingerly and held the door aloft for Raith, the Geflack walking as tall as a Geflack could marching from the room, never looking to the human to thank him for holding the door or indeed the food. Phobos did not like being treated this way and was not used to it, but the thought of more gold in exchange for the Myon made the Geflacks' ignorance much more bearable.

Phobos led the way with Raith following close behind and two as yet previously unseen guards followed a good distance behind. They walked in silence through dimly lit corridors heading to the centre of the human camp, Raith could tell they were getting close to the outside as the air became clearer and he could hear rain beating heavily against the floor. Daylight poured through an opening at the end of yet another corridor and the sound of rain was mixed with sounds of shouting and arguing, laughing and cheering from many different human voices. As they stepped outside the humans cheered at the sight of their leader and the mud squelched under foot, Raith liked this feeling as being inside a human camp was foreign to him and the mud between his lower fingers felt comforting. Phobos lifted his arms and welcomed the cheers; he grinned and turned to face Raith, silently saying how he should look how the humans love him so. Raith looked back with a blank expression he continued to scan the open area taking in all his surroundings. They had arrived at an arena and they were on a platform higher than all of the others. They were all shoulder to shoulder surrounding a huge mud and water filled pit, pushing and slapping each other for best position for the fights to come and to view their leader. In the centre a human was leaving via ladder after passing a half dead dog to his accomplice leaving the remains of some other beast slowly sinking in the mud in a red pool of gore and blood. Phobos moved forward to a large chair set out for him with a canopy so that he and his guests were sheltered from the elements, but still the whole area was spattered with pools of water and mud. He moved in front of his seat and motioned for Raith to come stand near his side which he begrudgingly obliged whilst the two following guards stood close by out in the rain, clearly not important enough to receive shelter from their leader. Raith scanned the crowd looking for the Myon, but could not see him anywhere, obviously the fights had begun but the main event was yet to commence and now they had arrived the Myon surely was to be brought from the bowels of this human dwelling. Phobos stepped forward to address his people and Raith stood silently on, watching and observing their behaviour with wry smile for the bloodshed to come.

Phobos: "Quiet! Quiet down I say! Today I have a rare treat for you men, today you will witness the most spectacular event since the long missed bear fights of years passed. Enter the pit, our three champions, the brothers of brutality, Roberson, Gelvin and Samson!"

The crowd erupted in screams of lust and fury, like mass demon possession on a monumental scale, Raith could not believe how deranged and unorganized Phobos allowed his people to be, pitiful he thought. Emerging from the crowds and making their way down ladders into the pit, three humans scantily clad in various items of leather amour, nothing matching or of correct size, still the humans thought themselves to be gods, drunk on the fame of the rabble that worshiped them, arms aloft as they turned from all angles bowing deeply to their admirers and pounding on their own chests to disperse their arrogance and as the cheers died the men turned to face Phobos and awaited his announcements.

Phobos: "And now, the challenger!! A creature thought long gone from our lands, strong as a mountain and as proud and vast as the everlasting sky... I give you... THE MYON!!!!"

The crowed bellowed angrily, roaring and cursing the air they spat and shook their fists in the confused celebration and from the furthest end of the pit the guards were parting the crowd, struggling to hold them back with spears as a barrier, the Myon was in sight, looking like an emaciated bear the Myon stood staring only at Raith. Through the insanity their eyes met and they were locked in hatred for each other, Raith smiled broadly and looked to the human, letting Ackrehm know he was in league with his captors and that he should abandon all hope. The Myon still stood proudly, his spirit still burned like a comet and he would never give up and never be slave to human or Geflack! Shaking him back to reality a guard sliced the ropes binding his feet with a flint blade then stood to hold his hand bindings, no sooner had he sliced them free Ackrehm was struck firmly in the centre of the back by a guard from the rear. Practiced and perfected in timing, the guard in the front was well out of danger when Ackrehm came flying forward heading face first for the bottom of the pit. He braced his fall with his arms, but with the rain turning this pit into a well he was briefly submerged in muddy water only to come bursting back out standing strongly to face his would be attackers. He quickly wiped the mud from his eyes, briefly looked up to Raith, then straight back at the humans that joined him in the pit.

Chapter 27.

The stockier man of the three shouted loudly in excitement and rage, he rushed towards Ackrehm swinging his fists wildly and uncoordinated at the Myon. Ackrehm struggled to move in the mud as it anchored his feet and clung on to him like a lost lover, but he could still out move the human. After dodging and then ducking under two punches the Myon timed a head tilt so a particularly wide swinging fist connected firmly with Ackrehm's unbroken horn. Shattering the bones, his attacker screamed, clasping his broken paw like a dog with a hornet sting, Ackrehm stamp kicks the human in his wide chest sending him soaring back through the air, landing winded and gasping for air on his shoulders and skidding into a muddy, windless heap gagging on mud and water as he struggled to breathe. After delivering his kick, another attacker grabbed Ackrehm round the waist from behind, clasping his own fist to seal the grip. The Myon broke the hold with his left hand by prizing the human's hands apart with his own thumb and levers the attacker's right forearm over his own. For a brief moment the human's arm bent before snapping abruptly sending a shard of broken bone piercing through the humans muddy skin and erupting a shrill scream that pierced the onlookers' ears just as the Myon had ensured his attackers own bone had pierced his own skin. Ackrehm quickly stepped forward creating space between his attacker and himself, still holding on to the splintered limb and spinning to face his attacker as he moved, the Myon supported the makeshift human dagger of bone with one hand and with a forceful shove of his attacker's bent wrist, skewered the human's stomach multiple times with pushes and pulls in quick succession.

Backing away from his dying foe, the Myon was kicked hard between the legs from behind, squashing his genitals against his own leg and sending a burst of sickness through his stomach into his throat and down all his limbs. Turning with watered eyes, the third human again tried for another groin kick only to be stopped short of his mark by Ackrehm's knee. In anger and pain the human swung ferociously attempting to pummel Ackrehm's jaw with hooking punches, but the Myon raises both arms and drops his chin allowing blows to rain and be absorbed on his forearms and biceps. Unyielding the attacker saw the Myon's open middle and shot in for a bear hug, but before he could flip Ackrehm over, he quickly dropped his elbows and in a pincer motion hooked both arms in at once so his fists could meet in the middle of his attackers soon to be shattered jaw.

When Ackrehm's fists almost met through his attacker's open jaw, the waist grip he strived for was lost and he stumbled back, groaning and drooling like a deaf mute with blood and his tongue spewing out of his limp sagging mouth. Head tilted back and his eyes to the heavens the attacker left his throat wildly exposed and vulnerable. A lightning right handed punch to the throat from the Myon split his windpipe and his cries, sealing his fate as he dropped to his knees and slumped to one side sending water and mud spraying and leaving the last few bubbles of air to disappear in the rain that came hammering down on its surface. Ackrehm approached the first attacker and offered an open hand to help him up, but sneakily the human slipped a blade from his ankle boot with his good hand and leapt from the ground to slice Ackrehm's inner thigh. Slipping in the mud the blade swipe fell a hair short of the Myon's leg and the attacker landed face down in the mud at his feet. Turning to look up the human in a panic and grinning nervously at Ackrehm only to see his disappointed and now sterile glare in return. The Myon kicked the attacker's hand sending the blade out of harm's way and the attacker's face back down in to the mud. Ackrehm then placed his foot on the back of the scoundrel's head, pushing his face deep in to the mud and water. Limbs thrashing frantically and fingers desperately clawing at Ackrehm's calf, the gurgles and mud bubbles slowed and then stopped. At that moment when the attacker's life had slipped away into the earth, the skies opened and cried torrential tears, drenching the Myon and washing the mud and all emotion from his face, turning towards the crowd the cries fell silent and the dripping and splashing of aqua cleansing were the only sounds to be heard through the deafening silence of the astounded onlookers.

Chapter 28
The Deal

Phobos and Raith had retired to the human's chambers and were drying in front of the fire, Raith sat on a stool closest to the flames, engulfing the warmth whilst Phobos paced behind him trying to catch the left over warmth Raith had spared him.

Phobos: "What a fight, hey, my friend, what did I tell you hey? Only the best I have for you good friend."

Raith: "The Myon might be good by human standards, but did you see that one? He's missing a horn! Hardly a prize is it?"

Phobos: "My friend, you jest surely, a horn, what is a horn?"

Raith span round to face the human, with the fire surrounding his figure, Raith looked as though he spoke truly form the depths of hell. "I never jest when in trade human and a Myon short a horn is like a king without balls to sire offspring, half as useful!"

"OK I'll admit he's a bit battered, but as we speak my men are cleaning him up for you, so might we speak monies my friend?"

Raith turned to face the flames, turning his back on the human continually showed he was really the one in charge and how Phobos hated him for this, but he had to maintain compliance and Geflacks were known for their wealth from engulfing so many villages so price should not be an issue despite being ruthless bargainers.

Raith: "I have left a bag of gold pieces on your table there, it is my offer, my only offer and there will be no negotiations, take or leave are your choices."

Phobos: "Well my friend this is very different to what I'm used to, allow me a moment to count please."

With trepidation Phobos emptied the bag on the table and was surprised at the generous sized gold pieces that poured out like an amber waterfall and scattered the table like stars in the night sky. Despite his inner gaiety, he thought best not to show this to the Geflack as he then may feel he no longer had the upper hand.

Phobos: "Oh really, but I felt he was worth more? Still you are wise my good friend and as I like you, I think we can agree on this amount, please excuse me I shall see to your purchase."

With that Phobos took his gold pieces slipping them one at a time back inside the leather purse and left Raith to the warm, stuffing the purse into his trousers so his men had no idea how much he had really gained. Raith knew he had over paid slightly for a slave, even if it was a Myon, but he knew how to manipulate the humans; their greed would always be their downfall and he was happy to exploit it. Truth be told even with the Cyclops skulking outside the camp ready to attack, chances of making off with the Myon unharmed would be slim, better to make the human think he got a good deal than to risk such a skirmish when the Myon was really the only piece of the puzzle that was needed.

Raith had begun to doze by the heat of the fire, it had lured him like the sirens that would lure travellers off in to the woods for murderous intent; he had given in to the warmth and it yoked his energy making his eyes give in to the promise of sleep. Suddenly he was awoken by the sound of human voices, shouting and cursing, the sound of metal chains clanging told Raith his newly acquired pet was on its way. With a quick bang, the door was struck then opened, bouncing of the wall with such force the wood sounded like it split. In a mess, one guard holding a chain leading to the Myon's bound wrists came stumbling into the room shouting for Ackrehm to 'keep back' and 'watch his step'. Following were two other guards with crudely made swords, rusted and bound with brown cloth, but against a bound prisoner they would suffice; then finally Phobos entered the room, he gave the guards and the Myon a wide birth making his way round to the Geflack.

Phobos: "Here my friend, as agreed, cleaned and dressed ready for transport. You won't regret it my friend, this one will make a fine gift for your king".

Raith looked daggers at the human, he had spoken of the plan to deliver the Myon to his king, this was something he would have like to keep to himself for a little longer at least, still no matter, the Myon was his and would soon be under control when under the watchful eye of the Cyclops and the others.

Raith: "Well now, at last we meet, quite a show Myon, have you a name?"

Ackrehm stood silent and proud like a stone carving, battered, bruised and almost eroded by time like cliffs by the sea; however hard he tried to he was refusing to show weakened signs of the hardships he had endured. Hands bound he stood clad head to toe in a mix match of skins and furs that the humans had fashioned for him, they had even bound his legs in leathers for protection as he was going to be a steed, the feet needed looking after.

Raith: "No? Well I'm sure we can think of a fitting name soon. Phobos you have done well, polishing up such a rough diamond. Please have him taken to the front gate; I am ready to leave at once."

"Of course my friend, as you wish. Men, take him to the front!"

With that the guards commenced shouting and yelling at the Myon, but it was quite clear he moved at his own speed and try as they might, their orders and venom did not pierce him in the slightest. They left the room and shortly after Phobos and Raith followed. When they reached the gates and outside, the wind had become icy, replacing rain with sleet and whipping across the land, lashing the faces of all whom endured it, the human guard which held the Myon's chain lead gingerly handed it to the Geflack then quickly retreated back to the safety of their fort.

Phobos: "Goodbye master Geflack, should you need to trades again remember me won't you, remember 'Phobos king of the slaves!!!!'"

Raith looked at the Myon and for a moment they both shared a thought, a feeling for the human leader that he was indeed a fool and spoke far too much. Without acknowledging the human's words, Raith turned and lead the Myon away from the fort, Ackrehm walked at his own pace and there was a loop in the chain as they trudged, Raith felt at ease he now had the prize he came for and Ackrehm just happier to see the trees and breathe such clean air again; filthy humans lived in squalor leaving their waste anywhere they chose and he was pleased to be away from them, however he knew that being with a

Geflack was not much better. As they trudged onwards the sleet turned to snow and it settled on their shoulders like the snow covered mountain tops. A rustling from ahead produced Arden, he stood in their way grinning with inane excitement at the Geflack and his pet Myon.

Lifting the chain and offering it at arm's length to the Cyclops, Raith saw to unburden himself of the Myon and such a menial task as a slaver.

Raith: "Arden, would you?"

Arden moved in and took the chain lead from the Geflack, Raith moved on to be leader once more and always in charge, Arden gave a sharp tug on the chain and sniggered to himself treating Ackrehm like a stray dog that had finally been retrieved and was at last being brought home to its master. As they all moved on, Toad appeared behind them carrying the groups things on his back wrapped in cloth to protect them from the elements with his club's handle hanging from the centre of the rolled mass, crunching the settling snow and forming ice under foot loudly so Ackrehm knew another had joined the group. Lastly, letting them pass her, Kornelija slipped silently from the trees and took up the position from the rear of the mercenaries. Onward they moved, not speaking or acknowledging each other in the slightest, just simply moving as one solid unit with its prize at its centre, the last Myon finally in their embrace.

Chapter 29

The group had been walking for a day and a night and after the second day were all feeling the fatigue; the bitter cold had chilled them all to their bones' core. As the light began to fade they approached a sheltered area that appeared to be felled trees years since passed leaning up against a rock face that could provide some shelter from the snow and wind. Toad went and set a fire and after warming himself with the flames and occasional sips from his personal drinking pouch, he moved away to allow others to absorb its strength-giving properties, but mainly to avoid any unwanted conversations that people felt the need to undertake amidst the pleasant silence. Arden had seated the Myon far enough from the flames that he felt no benefit and kept hold of the long lead whist he took up his familiar position next to Raith, acting as his wind shield and heat provider. Kornelija had momentarily dismissed all fears of betrayal from Raith and the others for now and the need to thaw overtook any other feelings. She passed the Myon to the flames and glanced at him, the cold was taking its toll, his head shielded by his long hair slumped exhausted on his knees as he balled himself up to fight off the cold. She watched as his breath rose through the snow covered branches, watched as his soul began to leave, what hardships he had endured she thought, he will die if she did not help.

She slowly rose to her feet and moved towards him, this had been the first time noise had come from her steps, fresh fallen snow crunching under her feet as she moved. She did not want to surprise the Myon, a wild animal although beaten and exhausted can still attack furiously if startled. As she moved graciously towards him, Toad opened one eye to glance in the direction of the noise, when he saw it was the Elf, he sniffed loudly and attempted to return to his dream. As she came but two paces from the Myon, Raith spoke from the darkness.

Raith and Arden had moved to a higher point on the low cliff edge so they could look down and observe the group and their prize from a bird's eye view and of course the added bonus of making Raith feel more king-like having aloft views of his small dominion.

Raith: "That one is not for talking to."

Kornelija: "He will be too dead to talk or anything for that matter if we do not warm and feed him."

Raith: "Very well, but dogs stay on their leads, for their own safety and others."

Kornelija: "Agreed."

Kornelija turned back to the Myon and he sat looking up at her, squinting from the falling snowflakes and from the struggle to see her face as she stood bathed in darkness with her back to the fire and the light it gave off.

Kornelija: "Please stand so that I may move you closer to the fire, can you stand?"

Ackrehm: "I can."

Struggling slightly due to cold and injury, Ackrehm fought the urge to look weak in front of his captures, they must never see they are winning, they must never know his sprit was being crushed every moment in their company, he needed rest and time to heal, but for now he must stay aware, he must escape.

Stepping backwards, Kornelija moved towards the fire and Ackrehm followed, ever closer he could feel the fire's warmth like he was dozing in the green, lush fields years from this cold place in the summer sun. He moved from her, shadowing the flames and sat on a thawed rock close to the fire so that his legs could feel every beam of light and heat. Kornelija placed an animal skin from her shoulders onto the earth beside him and sat arm's length, to observe his movements and also being closer to a prisoner was still preferable to the Geflack and the Cyclops. Arden still kept hold of the chain allowing it to pass through his fingers as the Myon moved, but still making sure it could be snatched taut in an instance. As Kornelija helped the Myon to stand she felt something hard and sharp under the back of his coat and as he moved she skilfully removed it quickly tucking it in to the back of her belt, but not before taking a quick glance to see it was a piece of deer antler, simple but a weapon none the less. She saw best to relieve him of this before he could find the strength to use it, possibly she thought what the humans had in mind all along, perhaps Raith had made more of an impression on them and they saw to arm the Myon as a little parting gift.

After at least two hours staring in to the flames, Ackrehm felt like the ice in his core was beginning to melt, but with that then came pain of all his injuries as the blood began to flow to them. Kornelija moved to reach for the poker handle emanating from the burning pile and stoked life back in to the dying embers whilst tossing on some loose nearby sticks Toad had already collected before moving away to sleep. Kornelija noticed colour had returned to the Myon's lips and cheeks, he looked tired and battered, but further from death's door than before. As the others were all snoring soundly, she decided she would find out more about their prisoner if he was indeed as dangerous as Raith would have them believe, she wanted to know about it.

Kornelija: "Myon... How old are you?"

Ackrehm did not turn to face her, simply continuing to look deep in to the flames, as if searching for the answer to her question in their dance around the wood and after waiting long enough for her to believe he was ignoring the question, in a deep but somehow tamed voice he replied, "Call me Ackrehm and I am sixty-four autumns."

Kornelija: "Yes of course! You may look that old, but I'm sure you are not."

Ackrehm: "My people age normally until about thirty, then the whole process slows; age is meaningless to me, as to an Elf I would imagine. We remain fitter, stronger and for longer than most races, but you wouldn't know that from our numbers."

Kornelija: "Are you the last?"

Ackrehm: (Sighs) "Possibly, I've not seen my like in autumns."

Kornelija: "Why do you say autumns? It sounds wrong."

Ackrehm: "My people seem to have young in the autumn, possibly why my race is strong, the first glimpse of life and we are plunged into cold, still my people are warm, or were."

Kornelija: "So your people are the result of the fruits of spring, fermented I mean."

He turned to her looking for insult, but she was smiling cheekily and he could not help feel warmer still from her joke.

Ackrehm: "Likely, still my mother was never around to confirm, she passed in birth along with my twin sister, my father and I spoke of many things, but my conception was not one of them."

They both smiled this time and glanced at each other then looking back to the flames, unaware Raith was awake and had been listening to their conversations. He grew uneasy at the fact they seemed to bond, he knew Arden was loyal to the death, but Toad was new and disgruntled at the world, he could leave any moment, should the Elf bond with the Myon, then this mission could fail and so close to accomplishment. Raith silently moved back to his position where Arden lay, he moved to the Cyclops's face and placed his lower hand over part of the sleeping giant's lips. His eye lid shot open like a crossbow bolt and it focused with speed on the Geflack, Raith spoke quietly but as always with command. "Steady my friend and open your ears."

Arden nodded silently in agreement and continued to lie perfectly still to await his orders.

Raith: "I am to leave for my camp tonight and return with reinforcements, the Elf wishes to undo us, but on my return I shall keep her as a plaything when the Myon is delivered. You will watch them closely my friend and should the Elf betray us, kill her but keep the Myon we need that one alive, understood?"

Again Arden nodded silently, Raith removed his lower hand and placed it back on the ground with the other; He looked at Arden and for the first time gave a smile as if he was pleased with him, little did the Cyclops know this was like a spider smiling to a trapped fly. Raith pulled up the hood of his cloak and moved off into the night taking care to tread lightly missing all the nearby bushes and twigs so as not to alert the others to his exit.

Chapter 30
Lust & Scars

Arden stayed in his position for a while then rolled over to face the fire, moving closer to the ledge from where they had camped, Arden could almost look directly down and still remain bathed in darkness, he could listen and observe in complete watchfulness undetected. As he steadied his breathing he listened to what they spoke of, trying to piece together the conversation and piece together if he could what he had missed.

Kornelija: "It's not the first time I've had to bow to a lesser; I was lashed for turning down a marriage proposal from a so called 'Noble' Prince, he was weak and felt his status owned him all. Drunk with rage and ignorance he bound me to a tree in the village, stripped and sliced me with a thin rapier Elf blade as a punishment for a made up insult. Others stood by and watched, fearful of receiving the same, I was forced to serve in his chambers as a worker or more accurately play thing! Until one evening when he slept I boiled honey and water till it steamed like a volcano and poured it over his face. His eyes resembled bowls of milk, and his face... A death penalty still hangs over my head. See we both have scars as a constant reminder for each other; only mine make me smile when I think of how he is now."

Ackrehm: "The Cyclops has many scars, to brandish such marks speaks of clumsy brute force, careless and unskilled and this speaks volumes of their kind."

Arden overheard all her story to the Myon, they were comparing scars now! What did they know about scars he thought anyway? Their tiny things like he had left over from skin worms. His battle scars were deep and vast covering his body like the glacier trails through the mountains and he wore them with ignorant pride. Arden was particularly interested in the part of the story where she was the Prince's play thing, he wanted her as his play thing, of course he knew his sheer strength would probably kill her, but he did not care, she would not be the first slim one to die from his lusts, plus he liked the sound of cracking a pelvis and much prettier than his own kind.

Moving away from the watch point, Arden returned to his previous sleeping place to sit with his thoughts and contemplate his next move.

Ackrehm and Kornelija had finished their conversations spreading from pasts to presents, failures to victories and now settled down for the night. Ackrehm had warmed to the core and felt drunk with the peace it brought, for the first time in weeks; even being prisoner he felt warmer and safe. Kornelija did her duties and continued to monitor the Myon from a slight distance allowing him time to sleep alone by the fire as she knew his future would hold further hardship and even death. As she watched him attempting to lay comfortably with his multiple injuries, she could not help but feel sorry for him. The last of his kind, imprisoned for that very reason to be kept as a pet, to pay for some imagined insult he may have caused, Raith and the other Geflacks were a disease and they were soon to extinguish the spirit of what could be the last of its kind. These thoughts played heavy on her mind, but covered in her cloak she eventually trapped these thoughts outside along with the cold from her make shift womb and drifted off into sleep.

Arden had been watching, standing so still amongst the rocks and trees that Kornelija had not even noticed him as she bedded down for the night close by. He had slowed his breathing exhaling only through his nostrils ensuring that his breath could not be evident even in this cold. The wind helped mask his breath and his scent and like a statue he stood and watched through his narrowly opened eye, he watched Kornelija move away from the Myon and he watched her settle in. He watched her observing the Myon and he watched her settle. She had pulled her cloak over her entirety, snow had begun to settle on her gently moving mound and even long after her breathing had become rhythmic and predictable, Arden continued to watch for he wanted to catch her unawares for what he had in mind.

Toad had been snoring a drunken noise for some time and the Myon was facing away closest the fire, Arden and Kornelija were alone, just as he had been wishing and waiting for. Arden felt sure that he could attack unchallenged, opened his eye wider to focus directly on his prey; he silently shook the snow from his head and face and began to breathe normally. Deep mists of stagnant breath left his lips and flowed through the branches like a river returning to a dry bed finding all the contours and quickest routes. He stood taller than before and had lowered his head looking menacing like a demon of myth and folk law, his gaze pierced her oblivious form and he decided the time was right to move in and claim his prize. He fought hard to withhold his excited trembling from the anticipation and arousal filling and boiling over inside his bulbous physique and like a stalking mountain lion he gently took a step forward, slipping his pointed foot in to the winter blanket, feeling through the snow with his toes to avoid crunching sticks that would alert her to his presence. Step after silent step he approached, like a mountain of horror casting a poison shadow over the land as he closed in on the sleeping Elf.

Her body rose and fell as she breathed like a boat gently bobbing on a calm canal and he studied her form obsessively, looking for where her breath mixed with the cold night air, he wanted to know where her head lie for the perfect attack. Elves are deceptively powerful and he would need to use his weight to overcome such a nimble and lightning fast foe, he looked for her head so he could judge where her limbs would be and then he could be in complete control. After mapping the event in his mind several times over, the smile began to take over his face, veins pulsated in his yellow swollen eye and drool had begun to cascade from his slightly open mouth and just before a droplet fell free from a freakishly large scar on his chin he fell forward, like a silent tree being felled and with arms outstretched he slammed on top of her sending an avalanche of snow skyward.

Chapter 31

Panic and pain awoke Kornelija as she struggled to breathe let alone move under what she first feared was a bear attack. She could slightly move one leg and kicked as hard as she could against the beast that had pounced, but to no avail. She struggled and fought quickly realizing this was no bear, her arms were pinned by the wrists and her face being crushed into the icy ground by a mass that seemed to snigger. As a voice spoke in soft malice the stench of rotten meat betrayed its owner and gave way to fear and panic of the attacker's identity.

Arden: "Got you now Elfy."

Kornelija traversed and grappled, clawing and biting at her own cloak attempting to injure the Cyclops, but her efforts against his elephantine size were useless and quickly she began to tire from the rage and exhaustion of his weight and his taunting laughter.

As Arden held the struggling elf to the ground, he began using his legs and hips to slide her cloak up towards her head. He wriggled and shifted, but always keeping his mass on top and ensuring never to let go of her arms and of course trying not to crush all the life out of her at once, just her fighting spirit would do for now. Slowly he managed to move the cloak higher and higher keeping her face and screams muffled from the others. She kicked frantically like a drowning child, but Arden had moved her arms together so he could hold both in one hand and was now using his free hand to stuff her cloak into her face and mouth. He could feel her warm stomach against his thighs as he straddled her and this seemed to only excite him more, her body acted like a drug and he was indeed a monstrous addict exploding with anticipation of the euphoria he was about to be engulfed in. With her head well and truly covered, her arms secure and her torso held fast by his chest, Arden began to feel down her body with his mammoth hand, rough and clawing as it moved marking her stomach in its wake. He trembled and panted like a rabid dog as she fought harder moving his fingers over her belt. Clasping it in his mighty fist he almost broke her back as he turned and twisted his fist, but luckily the leather gave way before her spine and just as he was releasing her belt and about to rip off her trousers, like a meteorite showing both Arden and Kornelija in flames and sparks, the Cyclops had been hit like a tidal wave across the back of the head and shoulder by a huge burning log wielded by the rarest of creatures. The Myon had attempted to split Arden's head like a block of lumber and had caused a noticeable dent in the back of the monster's skull. After nearly crushing the Elf to death and in a drunken daze Arden lifted his body up from his prey whilst holding the back of his head and attempted to stand, in the blink of an eye Kornelija had flung the cloak from her head and had produced the antler she had previously taken from the Myon and began to rain blows in to the Cyclops's throat, piercing his neck and windpipe multiple times showering her manic face in crimson rain as she went. As she hammered the life from her attacker a blade had appeared at her boot tip and she proceeded to attempt to remove any further threat this beast might have in the form of his member by attempting a brutal and frenzied castration.

Arden's body slumped to the side landing on his back in a twitching mass and the last quickening breaths began to labour and deepen until they stopped for good. His life left his gaping, blood filled mouth in the form of a cloud in the cold night air rising upward and then away in to the breeze. Kornelija had kicked herself away from the Cyclops, still shaking from fear and adrenaline she panted trying to control her emotions, staring deeply at her now dead attacker ready to attack again should life return to his corpse. Ackrehm walked closer to the Cyclops, standing over his body admiring the many puncture wounds he could now add to his scar collection. Ackrehm glanced at Arden's single eye, its pupil had shrunk to the width of a needle and it stared up at the night sky as if it had been attempting to follow his soul so as to not get left behind. A snowflake stuck to it and then dissolved almost returning life to it for a brief second in its moisture, but still his body remained still, he was indeed dead and no sorrow would be felt by any creature of this land.

In all the commotion and the fixation on Arden, Toad had mistakenly been forgotten. Ackrehm and Kornelija were still transfixed with the Cyclops and the moment that had come to pass, they were both oblivious to their surroundings and more importantly the Myon was unaware of the Dwarfen rage that approached. Toad had been observing the commotion from a safe distance, but now the mighty tree had been felled, he could approach in the confusion and make his mark. As the Myon had his back turned, Toad struck the base of his spine with the side of Emell's axe sending pain spiking through Ackrehm's brain and rendering him unconscious on his feet. Ackrehm slowly slumped forward landing face down on top of Arden sending the fear of death through an already emotional and panicked Elf. Kornelija could not see what had happened to the Myon until Toad approached and she could make out his bearded face through the snow.

Toad: "Now that we have finished, tie him up Elf!"

Kornelija simply looked in disbelief at Toad, desperate to see a glimmer of hope or decency in his eyes, but his soul was as dead as Arden, he had been hired to keep a Myon captive and that he would for the promise of gold was like an opiate to a Dwarf.

Toad: "Tie him I say or feel my axe Elf, I won't lose my gold for you or any!"

Kornelija shook the sense back in to her own mind and struggled to her feet, the shock had numbed her limbs, but the blood began flowing again and she became hypnotized in a trance of function rather than thought, ghostly she moved over to the Myon, holding the back of his clothing she dragged him away from the Cyclops and closer to the fire, still leaving him face down she bound his wrists with the lead he had previously been attached to and backed away, staring through his shallow breathing body in to a dream world of nightmare that shock and Arden had created for her. Toad stepped to her side and without looking at her spoke in a harsh and disrespectful tone.

Toad: "Now the one eye is done, you watch the Myon and I'll be watching you. We wait for the Geflack, understood?"

Kornelija did not answer however a response was not required, after his instructions he moved back to his previous makeshift bed and settled in, sitting with his back straight and his axe in hand he fixed his eyes on the Elf and did not plan to move his attention anywhere else. After a moment still looking at Ackrehm, Kornelija sat where she stood, wrapping herself in her cloak and observing the Myon as she had been told. Her mind raced with tormenting images of what could have happened had the Myon not come to her aid, had the beast had his way and now she had her hero captive, bound like a deer for slaughter; she questioned what sort of life lay in his future, what sort of life could anything have with Geflacks as rulers? The guilt of keeping him like this began to burrow in to her brain like woodworm; it tormented her almost as much as the memory of the Cyclops' stinking breath had burnt itself in her nostrils and mouth.

Chapter 32
Decisions

Neither the Elf or Dwarf slept and after several thought filled hours, the light began to bleed over the land from the sunrise, the snow fall ceased and the wind had dropped to a breath allowing the bounty hunters to loosen the grip on their cloaks. A loud crunching of sticks and branches was approaching fast causing the Elf and Dwarf to jump to their feet in unison, both with weapons drawn and scanning their surroundings frantically trying to pinpoint the location of this approaching threat. The Myon groaned drunkenly awaking from his forced slumber and still in obvious agony from Toad's strike. Kornelija jumped to his side and whispered to be silent as danger approached, he complied and lay still, hoping he could play dead in an attack then make good his escape when the danger was busy with the others.

Suddenly, bursting through a particularly thickly snow covered bush sending showers of sticks and snow in to the heavens, a mighty creature stood. Stocky and rather fat, but of a very tall build it stood, panting like an Ox from the obvious distance it had been running. Its head was bound in leather and metal, not even its eyes were visible from the mask so it was impossible to tell if these eyes were kind or dead inside. Suddenly peering over its helmet, holding on to straps and handles looking down on them with an arrogance they had only ever seen in Raith the Geflack, only this one was different. He clearly had been a leader for some time and he stunk of a superiority complex that Raith could only dream of. Quickly appearing at the two characters' feet, Raith appeared, struggling to not look out of breath he had clearly been laboured to keep up, he quickly composed himself and attempted to take command in front of Toad and Kornelija.

Raith: "You see my Lord; the Myon is here as promised."

Raith scanned the area looking for his pet, the Cyclops was key to his plan, but he could not be seen.

Raith: "Arden! Where is Arden?"

After a few moments silence Toad spoke up. "Dead! Decided to try having the Elf in the night, her and the Myon put him down. Who's this then that rides the beast?"

Kadamlic: "I am your employer Dwarf! You may address Raith, but not me directly! Raith! What has been going on here, you said you had control of everything, it seems in your absence, your 'Slavers' have run amok?!"

Raith: "High spirits King, still the Myon is here as you requested; see over there by the Elf."

Kadamlic climbed down from his mount and approached the Myon who had now turned on his side and faced his nemesis as he approached. Kornelija kept her position, but looked down toward the floor showing no threat and compliance to one so supremely arrogant. As he moved in Ackrehm pulled at his bindings in a furious attempt to check they were still firm and see if he could at last break free to choke the life from this creature that had caused him such torment and misfortune.

Kadamlic: "Well hello again Myon, you remember me don't you? As you can see my leg has healed, but you seem to be rather worse for wear. This won't do, my new horse must rest before he is broken in properly!"

Ackrehm: "You think I will carry you around like that thing on my back?! If your fool enough to try, so be it."

Kadamlic: "Still have fire I see, good, you will become obedient and controlled or I will trim off that last horn of yours!"

Ackrehm kicked out in anger, but he was too far away to do anything other than shower snow on the Geflack king. Kadamlic bent over looking down on the Myon and laughed, he had won and now had what he wanted, he would make this Myon a slave and keep him alive anyway he had to, in constant pain and destroy every last shred of spirit he had left. Ackrehm could read all this from his sickening laugh and could do nothing due to bindings and injury. Kadamlic righted himself and slowly turned to face Raith still grinning wider than a canyon with self-appreciation and in awe of future torments.

As the Geflack turned, Kornelija looked up from her crouched position and in a blink of an eye span round to face Toad. As she moved a silver glint caught everyone's eyes and her cloak flowed like a black river in slow motion behind her. She fixed her eyes on Toad and the look on her face had changed from emotionally damaged back to warrior Elf. Toad felt a fear wash over him and as he stared back at the Elf warrior he noticed outstretched in her hand, pointing to floor with a single drop of black liquid beading at its tip was one of her razor edged blades. Her cloak finally settled revealing Kadamlic clasping at his throat and Geflack blood spilling through his fingers. He swayed and coughed, desperately trying to speak, he turned to Raith and stumbled towards him pleadingly and falling to the floor, struggling in the quickly blackening snow like a fallen fledgling. Raith stood and grinned at the sight he had been longing for, the King was dying and his dreams of power could soon become reality.

Keeping her eyes branded on Toad, Kornelija moved like a stalking cat stepping over Kadamlic's body moving toward the Myon. She stepped over him to his back and slit the binds so precisely, he did not even feel her do so and it was only when the straps fell in to his palms he realized he was free.

Ackrehm mustered the strength to force himself to his feet and he stood at Kornelija's side, he could stand taller than before and he felt more alive than he could remember since the day that he and Therd had been crossing the forests and had run in to the Geflack disease. He towered above her, but her presence was that of the Cyclops's when he still breathed; she struck fear in to those that stood and even the most hardened solider would have questioned their next move. As their eyes met and they sized each other up in silence, Raith ever the manipulator, was of course the first to speak. "Elf, if you walk away, I will see you get your gold, and Arden's share, now I am King thanks to you, I can make it so."

Kornelija made no reply, but her looks of death were answer enough.

Raith: "Very well, Toad! Quell this rebellion and you shall be at my side and handsomely rewarded."

Both Ackrehm and Kornelija looked to the Dwarf who stood in fighting stance with his axe at the ready, but he halted, he did not advance.

Ackrehm: "Since when did a Geflack keep its word?! Do you even want to be puppet to this filth, since when were the Dwarfs slaves?"

Toad looked from Elf to Myon, contemplating his next move and weighing up his options.

Toad: "Dwarfs are leaders and I've followed this fool long enough, you are on your own Geflack."

Raith made no reply, but the three kept their eyes on each other until Toad began to lower his axe and they could tell the danger was lessening. Ackrehm was the first to turn to where Raith was stood, but he had gone, disappeared like a drop in the ocean, but leaving no ripples to follow.

Ackrehm: "He's gone, I might have guessed!"

When the Myon spoke, both Toad and Kornelija each turned to where Raith had stood and then looked around to see if they could spot his retreat. He was gone, like the devious coward he had slipped away when the threat became too real and without his bodyguard to speak in violence for him. Ackrehm and Kornelija had finished looking for Raith, satisfied he had gone they both looked toward Toad who had already collected his meagre possessions and without word had turned to depart through the snow, trudging off into the distance and not looking back.

Kornelija: "And him?"

Kornelija motioned towards the beast Kadamlic had ridden into their camp, it was looking around for its master and looking very lost. The Elf calmly approached whispering so quietly the Myon could not make out what she said, but the beast began to calm and on her drawing near it knelt and bowed its head. The beast was very large and if it wanted could cause serious injury, but under her influence it was as meek as

144

a new born. She slowly used her blade and began cutting the straps and binds to its helmet; Ackrehm approached also taking care not to startle the beast as like approaching a wild horse he could sense the possible fight or flight reaction to a sudden noise. As she cut the final leather belt she looked to the Myon and he stepped closer taking hold either side of the helmet and firmly lifting it free of the beast's head.

The smell of old meat and blood hit them even outside and the beast looked around frantically for guidance or help. They could see this was an Oaf of the hills, misshapen in its face from the binds that had been so tight for so long they could barely still tell what race it was. The normally gentle creature had been captured and beaten in to a two legged horse for the Geflack king and to add to the horror of treating such a gentle creature this way, they had also sewn its eyes closed. Kornelija placed her hand on the Myon's forearm and softly lead him to step back which he did still holding on to the helmet and fixated in disbelief. The elf with surprising speed nicked the threads that bound the Oaf's eyelids shut and it jumped to its feet blinking and turning its head from side to side, moaning and crying out for the light burned like embers in his eyes. Ackrehm went to pull Kornelija back out of harm's way, but she held her hand out motioning him to stop, she began to whisper again and even being much closer this time Ackrehm still could not understand what she said, not that it was in a strange language, but as though it was simply not meant for his ears. The Oaf calmed and its blinking began to slow, with its huge fingers it carefully pulled the remaining thread from its eyes; as painful as it must have been the beast made no sound and as it became accustomed to the light it looked at the Elf warrior and smiled a toothless simple, but childlike grin in thanks for her kindness. After a few moments of gleaming un-vocalized appreciation the Oaf turned and with a freedom previously unseen quickly began to walk and then run out of the camp heading back the way the group had travelled presumably in search of the hills from when its race hailed.

Ackrehm looked to Kornelija who was still watching the Oaf and he noticed a relaxing calm in her that he had not seen before, that act of kindness had softened her slightly and he could see that the Elf warrior was also as gentle as she was deadly.

The duo stood side by side for several moments of blanketed silence until without facing each other the Myon spoke. "Thank you."

"How could I let you be taken, after what you did?"

"It was only a normal reaction to help."

Kornelija: "And that's why your thanks are not needed, because you see what you did as normal in a world that is anything but."

Ackrehm: "What now?"

Kornelija: "Now I need quiet."

Ackrehm: "Well you are welcome to join me back to my cart, it's a long journey and I'm not a big talker."

Kornelija: "Sounds good for now."

Kornelija collected her shoulder bag and she sheathed her blade hoping not to have to draw it again for some time to come, the pair left the camp and the carnage behind them. Raith would most likely return to his tribe and claim the throne he so desperately wanted, he had no real reason to peruse them any further, but leaving this place so close to their camp was of course their best choice to make. And so they left, to return to Ackrehm's cart and his life as a simple trapper and trader; Kornelija would stick with him for now, she felt a safety and kindness with him that was a rare gem in this world and she felt proud to be in the presence of possibly the very Last Myon.